UPON THE MOON
AND WOODSTOCK

UPON THE MOON AND WOODSTOCK

Jeanie Bryson Clemmens

ReadersMagnet, LLC

Upon The Moon And Woodstock
Copyright © 2020 by Jeanie Bryson Clemmens

Published in the United States of America
ISBN Paperback: 978-1-951775-49-0
ISBN eBook: 978-1-951775-50-6

All rights reserved. No part of this publication may be reproduced, stored in a retrieval system or transmitted in any way by any means, electronic, mechanical, photocopy, recording or otherwise without the prior permission of the author except as provided by USA copyright law.

The opinions expressed by the author are not necessarily those of ReadersMagnet, LLC.

ReadersMagnet, LLC
10620 Treena Street, Suite 230 | San Diego, California, 92131 USA
1.619. 354. 2643 | www.readersmagnet.com

Book design copyright © 2020 by ReadersMagnet, LLC. All rights reserved.
Cover design by Ericka Obando
Interior design by Shemaryl Tampus

CONTENTS

Introduction 7

Chapter One: Moon Landing 11
Chapter Two 15
Chapter Three: Sports 20
Chapter Four: The rise of skirts and decline of the necktie 24
Chapter Five: Vietnam 28
Chapter Six: Hillary Rodham and collegiate views 38
Chapter Seven: The Peace Movement 41
Chapter Eight: A different sort of activism 47
Chapter Nine: Slang, Who sang, and Hope Lange 52
Chapter Ten: Woodstock and The Boy Scouts 57
Chapter Eleven: Older Americans 61
Chapter Twelve: Take Us to Cuba? 63
Chapter Thirteen: The Other Outer Space 65
Chapter Fourteen: 1969 Companies 71
Chapter Fifteen: ARPANET 74
Chapter Sixteen: Vital Statistics 77
Chapter Seventeen: TV, Toys, and Talk Shows
        (with commercials, of course) 79
Chapter Eighteen: Poverty Wins? 83
Chapter Nineteen: River Fire, Oil spill, and other happenings 85

Chapter Twenty: Tax Reform–Boring Alert 88
Chapter Twenty-One: Guns 90
Chapter Twenty-Two: Future Billionaires 92
Chapter Twenty-Three: Some things don't change much 96
Chapter Twenty-Four: You don't get more
 "back to the land" than farms 99
Chapter Twenty-Five: Flower Children, Body Art,
 and Patchouli 102
Chapter Twenty-Six: Guitars and Sitars 104
Chapter Twenty-Seven: Education and 'Saving' TVPBS 106
Chapter Twenty-Eight: Religion in 1969 109
Chapter Twenty-Nine: Inventors and Scientists 112

Summary 119
Notes 121
References 124

INTRODUCTION

"The Eagle has landed" was arguably the most significant sentence in 1969, followed closely by "One small step for man, one giant leap for mankind". History records July 20, 1969, when Neil Armstrong walked on the Moon, as the greatest moment of that year. It was the culmination of years of engineering work and the dedication of scores of scientists and astronauts.

I joined in the celebration of victory that July, but personally for the most part I didn't have much nostalgia for 1969 as I began this book. The deluge of social issues, consciousness-raising, technological innovations, and exotic philosophies that bombarded me, during my first year at college were a little overwhelming. I suspect it was that way for many young people in 1969 as "every protest, every dissent" was an attempt to forge an identity in this particular age", as Hillary Rodham said in her Wellesley commencement speech. At colleges and universities across the country, those attempts sometimes took the form of protests that sometimes turned violent and sometimes caused property destruction. (See more in Chapter 7). I suspect that if you carried a sign that only said "UNFAIR" onto most campuses in 1969, you'd draw a crowd that agreed with the unfairness of administration policies; dorm rules; government; parents; war; discrimination against blacks and women; animal experimentation; the plight of farmworkers or more. Being against things was big then. But only remembering the turbulence, rebellion, and discord does 1969 a great disservice. Many books about this period in history (excluding those about the Vietnam War, the Moon Landing, and Arpanet) use the term "late sixties to early seventies" without regard to the effects of events and people in the individual year.

1969 was unique in many ways and not just about protest and hippies. Rebelling against parents and their lifestyles, challenging authority and established values is not unique to 1969 and is not a focus of this book. I use the broader term counter-culture, which includes hippies but is not limited to that group. Without ignoring the counterculture, it shouldn't be forgotten that there were astronauts, inventors, and businessmen; senior citizens, babies, and school children; musicians, athletes, and artists; academic scholars, and trade school students learning to fix furnaces, pipes and electrical wiring; drinkers, drug users, and abstainers too. Dedication to work, humor, values, and fun were part of that year as well.

More research convinced me that 1969 was crammed with events that were far-reaching and as diverse as the people who lived then and today. Many things that happened in that year are not in most history books but are part of the overall picture of life then. This book is not political, nor is it a memoir, although on two or three occasions I make a comment. 1969 may not have been a pivotal point for either the Vietnam War or changes in society; however, many of our views and habits today are the resultant vectors of 1969 "arrows" pointing toward the future. The tips of those arrows were seeds of change, planted individually or collectively toward specific targets.

If 1969 were a fruit, it would be a pomegranate–ordinary looking on the outside, but filled with scores of edible seeds, each one with the potential to affect the future with its growth. Some seeds, ARPANET and the back to the land movement, would sprout into the Internet and the organic farming we have today. Others, like Ralph Baer's patent for playing games on television, would become young people's favorite pastime. The civil rights, feminist, green, and "lower the voting age movements" would grow, effectively educate, and bring enlightenment. America expanded its knowledge in computers while Pele scored his 100th soccer goal and the Concorde took its first flight in France. 1969 brought our country national pride in space; and an international disgrace with Lt Calley's trial, revisiting the My Lai massacre in Vietnam.

In the spring of 1969, teenagers were like those of today, focused on the prom and getting used to the idea of going to college or working full time. The girls worried about what their hair looked like to the boy who sat three rows behind in trig class after he'd asked her to the dance. The boys had bigger concerns with the draft and Vietnam. This is not to say that the girls were just frivolous and egocentric. The war wasn't quite as real to them as yet. As the months went on and friends were "called up", they became more concerned, of course. Some people thought that America was in deep trouble in Vietnam, but the walk on the Moon was a tremendous boost to national pride. NASA astronauts had done something no one else had ever done. (Take that, Sputnik!). Though the United States wasn't winning in Vietnam, at least we had beaten the Russians to the moon.

It was a year as much about Breck shampoo and long beautiful hair as it was about "flowers in your hair", as much about Johnny Carson and Sesame Street as about music festivals. My dentist was 16 and was hit by a car in 1969, suffering a concussion and long treatments. A Facebook friend was a young wife raising small children and working in an office that didn't treat women as equally as men. The baritone next to me in choir is a Navy Veteran (Vietnam/Gulf of Tonkin) who bought his first house that year. A middle-aged couple from my traditional church quit and then joined a commune. My husband was in a national fraternity at an almost all-male engineering school, favoring 50's music (Beach Boys, Jan and Dean, etc.), beer, and car racing over rock, drugs and Volkswagen buses. My beloved grandmother was 89 and lived independently. So, being comprehensive became important to me. If something happened in 1969, I researched it.

 The standout events like NASA's triumph in space and The Vietnam War dominate most published works that include 1969. However, the focus of this book is primarily everything else that happened in 1969 and is limited to only that year (with a few exceptions used as background or follow-up) and America. The referenced facts reflect, but do not necessary define or explain, the mood of the country, at the time. If anything, 1969, was a year of movement; non-static processes of thought and change, which were ongoing into later decades. I invite you to read on to find out what many other Americans were doing in 1969 and what influences spilled over onto later generations.

CHAPTER ONE

MOON LANDING

1969 was so long ago that over half of the current population wasn't even born yet. Most of them, however, have waited in an airplane or bus seat, about to make a journey to somewhere new, hoping that the trip would be smooth. Imagine how it would feel to sit in a 7.6 million pound space vehicle about to make a 952,700 nautical mile journey to the moon and back, a 195-hour trip. So many technical things had to go right for the Apollo 11 mission to be successful.

- The first stage of Saturn V's (launch rocket) engine had to ignite (followed by the four other engines) and the hold down clamps release for lift off from Cape Kennedy, Florida.

- Apollo 11 needed to jettison the first two stages and enter a 103 nautical mile orbit around the earth.

- About three hours later, a third stage engine was to fire to boost the spacecraft out of orbit and onto a lunar trajectory at 24,200 miles per hour. The astronauts had to successfully "unpack" the Lunar Module, Eagle, from its compartment atop the launch rockets. That required firing some explosive bolts to separate Columbia (the command ship) from an adapter and blow apart the four panels of the sides holding the LM. Once loose, the astronauts stopped the LM and docked it head to head with Columbia. They dumped fuel from the 3rd rocket stage to send it out of Apollo's path and continue toward the Moon.

- Earth's gravitational pull was used to slow the craft to 7,279 ft./sec and course correction had to be made when needed.

- Astronauts were required to sleep, perform duties (charging batteries, dumping waste water, checking fuel and oxygen levels), and make telecasts in cramped quarters for three days.

- On July 20, 1969, Aldrin and Armstrong crawled into the LM (no seats) to power it up. The two stage Lunar Module was comprised of a descent and ascent stage. Both were checked carefully. The first stage had to land them safely and the second stage had to get them back to the Columbia after the mission.

- A 20,500-pound thrust engine, fired for six minutes, exactly, functioned to slow the vehicle so it could be captured by the moon's gravity. Surveys of the moon's surface confirmed the landing site previously picked from the maps and photos provided by Apollo 8 and Apollo 10 missions. The spacecraft, which was behind the moon at this point, was without radio communication.

- The Eagle now had to successfully separate from Columbia and begin descent to the lunar surface. Mike Collins, alone in Columbia orbited the moon for two days. For 47 minutes every two hours he had only his tape recorder to talk to because he was behind the moon.

*Armstrong, piloting the Eagle, was forced to throttle and avoid a crater the size of a football field. Steering closer to their target, Aldrin gave altitude readings as Armstrong flew. They flew feet first and face down. Aldrin spoke, "picking up dust" as they came close to the ground and finally "Contact light. Okay, engine stop". The 68" probes below 3 of the 4 footpads were turned on and signaled with an indicator light on the instrument panel. Armstrong tells Mission Control "The Eagle has landed."

*Portable life support equipment weighing 84 lbs. on earth, but only 14 lb. on the Moon were strapped on and Commander Neil A. Armstrong opened the LM hatch, squeezed through, and descended the nine step ladder outside. On the second step, a D-ring was pulled to deploy a camera to film in front of him. He placed his left foot on the Moon's powdery surface and said, "That's one small step for a man, one giant leap for mankind."

- In 2 and a half hours of EVA (extra vehicular activity) much needed to be accomplished. The astronauts collected rock specimens, placed two devices to be left on the moon; a laser-reflector to make precise distance measurements and a seismic detector. They planted a 3 X 5 ft. nylon U.S. flag on the surface. Showing how detail oriented the mission team at NASA was, the flag had the top edge braced by a spring to keep it extended on the windless Moon.

- After 20 hours on the Moon, the astronauts needed to prepare to leave. Americans had seen some miraculous things on TV up to this point, but collectively worried that the astronauts would have difficulty coming back. The ascent engine on the LM had to work perfectly and so did the navigation and docking with Columbia, still orbiting with Michael Collins at the helm. A mistake could leave Aldrin and Armstrong stranded on the Moon, or worse, in outer space. Fortunately less than four hours after lift off from the moon, the Eagle (minus the descent stage and some other things left behind) docked with Columbia on the backside of the Moon.

- Not home yet, the astronauts ate, slept, and made television transmissions to Earth. They needed a successful separation of the command and service modules, safe re-entry into Earth's atmosphere, and an accurately placed splashdown to end their journey. Eight hundred twenty-five miles southwest of Honolulu, the U.S.S. Hornet picked them up. They were sprayed with disinfectant and then climbed up onto the flight deck of the ship. Nixon greeted them saying, "This is the greatest week in the history of the world…" NASA issued a statement that this was the "most trouble-free" mission to date; successful in every respect.

President Nixon spoke to the Apollo 11 astronauts when they landed on the Moon. He said it had to be" the most historic telephone call ever made." And he added "As you talk to us from the Sea of Tranquility, it inspires us to redouble our efforts to bring peace and tranquility to Earth. For one precious moment, in the whole history of man, all the people on this Earth are truly one." Neil Armstrong responded, "Thank you, Mr. President. It's a great honor and privilege for us to be representing not only the United States, but also men of peace of all nations…"

That peace was not to be just yet. Men still fought in Vietnam and there was growing civil unrest in America. But Nixon was correct about one thing at least, for one moment as Buzz Aldrin and Neil Armstrong stood listening, at attention, on the Moon, after planting the U.S. flag, America was united in a pride and purpose that will be remembered as unparalleled in that remarkable century.

CHAPTER TWO

Of course Americans rejoiced at the Moon landing news, but what were they doing in their lives before and after that? Not counting the lives of soldiers, college students, and toddlers, families lived a lot like today. Moms went shopping, dads went to work and kids went to school. Mom had a new place to shop for kid's jeans when GAP opened its first store on August 21, 1969. The new store also sold LP's (and please don't make me explain about old vinyl records). From the clothing store, the housewife probably went to the grocery store. She picked up Chiffon margarine, Campbell's Manhandlers soup, some tuna, Pillsbury Create-a-cake mix, Nestlé's chocolate bits and Cool Whip. She also tried out some products that were new in 1969–Kaboom cereal from General Mills, Frosted mini-wheats (Kellogg) and Pringles from Proctor and Gamble. She might have been planning to make Choco-Scotch or Sticks 'N Straws cookies or Topsy-Turvy Pineapple cake. If she didn't have one, she wished for an Amana Radar-range Microwave oven for "flameless electric cooking. At a cost of $495, chances are she couldn't afford one yet, but at least she had a portable broiler oven (toaster) and an electric skillet.

The Bureau of Weights and Measures or What does this government agency have to with shopping in 1969?

It's necessary to include two consumer events from a few years prior to 1969 to understand the relevancy. First, the Fair Packaging and Labeling Act passed in 1967 required that all packages be labeled with the weight. Second, Ralph Nader, aide to Secretary of labor, Daniel P. Moynihan, wrote a book, <u>Unsafe at Any Speed</u>, in 1967, which alerted consumers to the dangers of a car, the Corvair. My brother had one and the radio blared when you hit a bump–funny wiring. Anyway, Ralph Nader had some influence and people in later years started thinking that inferior products like the Corvair might be cheating them. When that cautiousness mixed with the new grocery store labels, there was trouble.

The Bureau of Weights and measures held a conference in June of 1969 and one of the speakers was Mrs. Margaret Dana from the Consumer Relations Counsel. She mentioned Nader's influence on people "who think they're being cheated every time they buy a package of food…" She had examples of consumers who had lodged complaints. One women said that she was charged for more than 2 lb. 4 ounces of meat even though the label said 2.40 lb. Margaret explained to her that the decimal point 4 was for how many tenths of a pound. She actually got 2 lbs. and 6.4 ounces. Another buyer bought 5 fl oz. of perfume but at home it only measured one tablespoon. Margaret investigated and found that the label said .5 ounces. Even today, consumer math teachers have difficulty getting this point across to students. Mrs. Dana also recommended the label "drained weight" when she found a 7 ½ ounce can of clams had only 3 ¾ ounce of actual seafood.

Mrs. Dana called the Fair Packaging and Labeling Act "one of the biggest steps forward in our national history." It's all about perspective, isn't it? There is one other thing that is a carry-over from that convention. The Apparel Research Foundation heard many complaints from women that clothing sizes weren't standardized, causing women to have to constantly return ill-fitting clothes. One gentleman in the audience suggested that women bureau employees try on the clothes to work on that. I suppose it got a laugh, but Mrs. Dana said some of them agreed to do it.

MEALS

Ethnic diversity being what is was then and now, there was variety at family dinners but more limited to Italian, German, Irish, and

French fare than Thai, Japanese, and Mexican cuisine. The 50's had been big on casseroles but not so much in 1969, although the ease of one-dish meals still had appeal. Americans ate at different times as well, usually dependent on dad's work schedule. But most families enjoyed a meal out. The usual places could now be replaced with two new chains which opened in 1969–"Wendy's" and "Long John Silvers Fish 'n Chips". Another new attraction at restaurants was the salad bar. There's no clear-cut winner in the "first salad bar" category, but during 1969 various places started to offer an array of vegetables for salads and salad dressing along with the meal. The practice was a way to keep the customer happy and busy while they waited for the rest of the meal. Salad bars became so popular that restaurants had to come up with a fair price for just the salad bar.

Also popular during that year was soul food. Bog Jeffries of "The Soul Food Cookbook" described it–"While all soul food is southern, not all southern food is soul." Increasing black awareness made soul food, like beet, collard, and turnip greens. almost a fad.

Picnics were as popular as ever. Party burgers, foil meals, and shish kebabs graced the backyard grills at many homes. Serving potato salad or tossed salad in wooden bowls was as common as ice cream with Kraft caramel or other toppings for dessert. Family gatherings featured iced tea, lemonade, and punch while the drinking crowds served Wolf Schmidt Clam diggers, Seagram's Royal, or Martini and Rossi Vermouth. The back cover of the June 20th Life Magazine shows Johnny Carson and a Saint Bernard in a blizzard. The caption reads, "Stir up a blizzard with Fresca and Smirnoff.

The space program had an influence on food choices as well. Tang, a juice product, was made available to consumers. Only the orange flavor was sold whereas the astronauts had a variety of flavors in the spacecraft. Also Space Sticks in peanut butter and chocolate flavors were sometimes included in care packages to college students from mothers who worried about the nutrition of their sons and daughters. They were not used or sanctioned by astronauts and my recollection of them is that they tasted a little like candy, but not really sweet. In their two meals on the moon, astronauts Aldrin and Armstrong ate bacon squares, peaches, sugar cookie cubes, pineapple-grapefruit juice and coffee for one; and beef stew, cream of chicken soup, date fruit cake, and orange drink for the other.

COST OF LIVING

That Amana Radar Range (first microwave marketed in the U.S.) cost $495 in 1969. A Zenith Color Console TV could be purchased for $498. But a "no-defrost", 16.6 cubic foot refrigerator-freezer sold for $309.95 according to an ad in The Chicago Tribune (Dec 4) that year. That same issue advertised mink and fox trimmed suits for only $67 and you could buy bell-bottomed pants and a silky blouse for $10.

New products such as the West Bend Popper, Kroger's new instant coffee jar that measures out a cup exactly, Bugles, Cracker Jacks, and Glad Disposable Trash Bags hit the market. Playtex introduced a first day tampon and the Toyota Corona hardtop was advertised at the "#1 lowest price" of $2135. Chevrolet started a drive for the youth market to sell its Camaro and Chevelle models, signing O J Simpson to make appearances at car shows. This was before he signed with the NFL. One forty-five-piece set of bone china (Rosemont green and gold on white) sold for $129.50.

An average bi-level house ran about $41,000 when new. Other custom built homes such as a new 3-bedroom ranch ranged from $17,793 to $24,990. Some sources use $15,500 for the average house cost in 1969 but it depends on the type of house, of course. Furnished apartments (in Chicago) were in the $111 to $140 range and up per month. For a car to park in the driveway, singles and families paid $2000–$3000 for a Lemans, Pontiac, Grand Prix, or Ford Squire Wagon but had to shell out $6695 for a new El Dorado and even more for a Mercedes or Jaguar. Several sources cite $8,389 as the median income in 1969 and even though some use a higher figure, it wasn't enough for most cars or other luxuries. Travel from

Chicago to Reno was only $21.96 round trip, but two weeks in Hawaii cost $599 and three weeks in Europe was $743 and up.

The following prices were common:

- Frozen veggies 6/$1 (broccoli, cauliflower, and brussel sprouts were 4/$1)

- Beer–Schlitz 12 12oz. $1.89, Miller High Life 24 bottles $3.57

- Scope Mouthwash—$.97

- T-bone steak—$1.29/lb.

- Baby Doll pajamas—$8

- Children's clothes at Zayre's or Sears—$1.50–$3.00

- Tuition at Harvard—$2,000 per year

- Movie ticket—$1.50

CHAPTER THREE

SPORTS

Who was the old man in the flamboyant fur coat in on the coin toss at Super Bowl XLVIII? Joe Namath, winning quarterback of the New York Jets at Super Bowl III, in 1969, is still setting style and strutting his stuff. Beating the Baltimore Colts 16-7 in Super Bowl III brought him instant fame, but Broadway Joe, as he was named, almost quit football. In 1969, he was part owner of a Manhattan nightclub called Bachelor III. The NFL Rule 3 was that players must not associate with gamblers or other notorious characters. Such people frequented Bachelor III. Super Joe was ordered by Football Commissioner Pete Rozelle to sell his interest in the club or quit playing football. In Namath's defense there were other players and owners who were either owners of clubs or connected with racetracks that weren't singled out and Namath said he didn't know about what went on at Bachelor III, especially when he wasn't there. The police verified that activities by frequent club goers, like Tea Balls, Snake, and Harry the Hawk, increased when Joe was away and dwindled to nothing when he was around. Still, on June 4, 1969, Joe Namath announced, "I'm not selling. I quit." He was giving up a $100,000 salary and he was only 26 years old. Namath eventually did sell his interest in the nightclub and returned to the Jets later that year.

Other Sports that year:

- World Series—Mets defeated Baltimore 4-1 (Bad year for Baltimore)

- Stanley Cup—Montreal over St. Louis

- NBA—Boston won over LA Lakers

- Kentucky Derby—Majestic Prince (also see women jockeys below)

- Wimbledon—Ann Jones trumped Billie Jean King and Rod Laver won men's)

- NCAA Football—Texas was best with 11-0-0 record
  NCAA Basketball—UCLA over Purdue (92-72)

  Boris Spassky became the World Chess Champion

On November 6, 1969 there was a buzzer controversy that resulted in an unprecedented replay of game. The Bulls (vs. Hawks) were denied the basket to tie the game when final buzzer sounded. The timekeeper said he hadn't touched the buzzer. Following an official protest by the Bulls General Manager, the request to replay the entire game was granted. The Bulls lost anyway, 142-137.

20-year-old, Diane Crump was the first woman jockey to race at a major track (Hialeah, FL) That same month, Barbara Jo Rubin, who had suffered childhood polio, was the first woman to win at a major track (Charlestown, WV)

SPORTS ILLUSTRATED AND THE SWIMSUIT ISSUE

$100,000 a year seems like nothing for a quarterback, but it was real money then. Players made enough for some to buy drugs, unfortunately, and the June 23rd issue of Sports Illustrated featured the threat of drugs–mostly amphetamines, steroids, painkillers, and muscle relaxants. One sport where you rarely heard about drug use was golf. Arnold Palmer turned 40 in 1969 and Lee Trevino and George Archer were at the top of their game. Speaking of game, the outdoor issue of SI was about the extermination of the grizzly bear. A later issue touted Ali-Clay as the undisputed king of the boxing ring.

In the college arena, basketball was hot. Pistol Pete Maravich was the LSU hotshot and Lew Alcindor, before he changed his name to Kareem Abdul Jabbar, heated up the UCLA court. In the NCAA championship, UCLA beat Purdue. Over in Texas, James Street ran a touchdown and the Longhorns streaked past Arkansas to win that NCAA tourney.

Despite belief that America's youth were suffering moral decay in 1969, the swimsuit issue in January that year was almost modest. Featuring a slim girl in a relatively small, purple bikini top and a mid-thigh colorful red, yellow and purple skirt, it was tame by today's standards. The cover caption read, "rich-nicks" in Puerto Rico" and upper arm jewelry and a fringed scarf glamorized the girl's outfit, while a male with a surfboard in the background hinted at the leisurely activities of the wealthy. Beatniks of the 50's and peace-nicks of the 60's gave way to what we called rich hippies or rich-nicks. The November issue, "Ski Italy", was devoted to those wealthy pleasure seekers who traveled.

Other great names in sports included Bobby Orr of the Boston Bruins and Vince Lombardi, coach of the Packers. More infamous, now, than famous was O.J. Simpson of the Buffalo Bills, who was twice featured on magazine covers that year–but only for football, of course, since this was long before he ran through airports or was accused of murder. Notable teams were the Minnesota Vikings, the Kansas City Chiefs and believe it or not, the Cleveland Browns.

As celebrations go, the ticker tape one in New York City after the Mets' victory was the biggest ever. On Wall Street some valuable records were thrown out the window along with all the paper. A bank worker at the Irving Trust Company was seen searching through the four-inch deep layer of ticker tape saying, "Half of this stuff is today's run–we're going to have to do it all over again."

Joey Cabell won the fifth annual Duke Kahanamoku Surfing Competition at Sunset Beach, Hawaii. Billabong Pro replaced the competition in 1985.

Arthur Ashe, who was the first black tennis player to win the U.S. Open (1968), turned professional in 1969.

The two Americans who made the 1969 Guinness Book of World Records that year were:

Charles Winfield, 19, at St. Mary's University, San Antonio, Texas For eating 210 goldfish on February 7, 1969

Guy Mudd, 32, at Dennison's Barber Shop, Kirkwood, Missouri for non-stop barbering (46 hours, 30 minutes) March 5–7 1969

CHAPTER FOUR

THE RISE OF SKIRTS AND DECLINE OF THE NECKTIE

Partygoers to a late sixties theme event could have a field day with fashion from 1969. Of course, there were bell-bottomed pants, granny skirts, and tie-dyed clothes but the mainstream population that year wore many fashions that were not so "hippie" designed. The mini-skirt was popular and was seen in many elegant forms. Also long pantsuits and skirts were popular. Here's the scoop on skirts:

The Hemline Index of George Taylor (1926) and the newer Skirt Length Theory both associate the direction of the stock market with the length of women's skirts. When consumer confidence is high and the stock market is going up, short skirts are in fashion; in times of gloom, as a bearish market, hemlines head down. Although the miniskirt was popular in 1969, so were midi and maxi skirts (granny skirts). From a strong market in 1968, stocks began declining in early 1969 and there was an attempt by fashion designers to put women in longer skirts, but women resisted being dictated to and wore what they wanted. With a new administration and possible peace in Vietnam there was confusion in finance and fashion. Perhaps that's the reason why the schizophrenic look of a maxi-coat with a miniskirt underneath was popular. Or maybe women just wanted to be fashionable and to keep warm.

A comment attributed to journalist Linda Ellerbee is "How intelligent is it to start the day by tying a noose around your neck?" Apparently some men agreed because a counter-trend in the 60's discouraged the use of neckties completely. Fashion designers like Ralph Lauren showed collarless open-necked shirts or polo-necked sweaters. For formal occasions and business, men still wore neckties, although they were much wider than in the 50's.

Not to be indelicate, but some women still wore girdles and stockings but they just didn't work with short skirts. The big news was pantyhose, which were comfortable with any style of dress. Only a few women were comfortable without wearing a bra, though. Dresses, coats, and suits, especially, were available in many new fabric materials too. The flowing styles were easy to sew with patterns from McCall's, Butterick, and Simplicity.

Progressions from the ban of DDT to public outcry against animal experimentation lead to fewer clothes with animal fur, but mink coats were still sold for around $300. The "scooter skirt look was popular too.

Skip through summer in
SKOOTERS

Wedding fashions ranged from long, simple granny dresses to elaborate lace or velvet gowns. Susan Chapman Molonson chronicles a description of a rich wedding at a resort in 1969 in her book, <u>Wentworth-By-The-Sea</u>. As a server, she describes, "small bunches of ivy and miniature roses" in a globe on the table "with maroon napkins." The meal started with "Lobster Bisque and then wild rice and mushroom stuffed Cornish Hens and asparagus tied with pimento 'bows'". The cake had "floral confections and molded marzipan doves" It was almond-flavored. The eight bridesmaids arrived in two limos wearing "hooded maroon velvet capes". The Bride's gown was "encrusted with pearls and sequins" with a "dangerously low scoop neck".

In contrast was a hippie wedding in Golden Gate Park where the groom wore blue velvet bell-bottoms and beads and the honeymoon was a walk through the zoo. Friends and family supplied food and drink. A photo of another hippie wedding depicts a bride in a long sleeve dress with necklace and a bouquet of flowers. The groom wore a long white robe and his hair was curled and long. Yet another wedding at a fire hall showed guests in casual dress (Van Morrison T-shirt, CPO shirt, or beads and sweaters) wearing canvas strap shoes.

Of the fashion models in 1969, Naomi Sims reached the top of the list that had previously featured Jean Shrimpton, Penelope Tree, and Verushka by becoming the one of the first African American super models. Born in Mississippi but a native of Pittsburgh and attending Westinghouse High School she went on to grace the covers of Time, Cosmopolitan, and the October 17, 1969 issue of Life magazine. Still around in 1969 were models Patti Boyd, who married Beatle George Harrison and Donyale Luna, who was the first African American cover girl, although not with the supermodel status of Sims. Other fashion models included Linda Morand, a Jackie-O look-alike, Peggy Moffitt, and Ali MacGraw, best known as the award winning star of the movies Goodbye Columbus (1969) and Love Story (1970).

CHAPTER FIVE

VIETNAM

I attended a panel discussion sponsored by the University of Pittsburgh Honors College with the theme, "Vietnam: New Lessons from an Old War". I hoped to learn as much as possible about Vietnam from the reporters, authors, U.S. Senator, and experts that were speaking.[1] I came away realizing that Vietnam, not being a decisive war, brought about more questions than answers. Involvement in Southeast Asia went back to the Truman Administration (1950–52) and continued until 1975 with the fall of Saigon. And while some experts believe it was a winnable war, some disagree. Daniel Ellsberg, who will be discussed in a later section, said in the DVD, "The Most Dangerous Man in America", that "It wasn't that we were on the wrong side; we were the wrong side." However, 91% of the Vietnam Veterans who saw heavy combat say they were proud to serve and would serve there again.

TROOPS

In 1964, 23,300 troops were stationed in Vietnam and by 1968 that number increased to 536,100. Escalation seemed to be slowing in 1969 when troops in Southeast Asia numbered 475,200, but on April 30, 1969 the war's peak troop strength was 543,482. That year, the Gates Commission was formed to advise President Nixon on an all-volunteer army. Their report wasn't issued until 1970. On December1, 1969, though, the lottery was established to rank all eligible men, born from 1944 to 1950, by giving them a supposedly random number: The lower the number, the greater the chance of being drafted.

The days of the year (1-366) were written on slips of paper, placed in separate plastic capsules, mixed in a shoebox, and then dumped in a deep glass jar. The capsules were drawn out one at a time. If you were thinking this was a primitive way to assign numbers, many mathematicians would back you up. Random number generators and computers like those of later generations weren't available. The unfortunate male born on September 14 got #1 from the first pick and the lucky guy born on June 8 got the last one. To this day, most men can recall their draft number as easily as their name. The choices were limited for those with low numbers but acceptance, volunteering for other branches of the service, draft dodging in Canada, and applying for conscientious objector status were among the options. Two of the speakers at the Vietnam panel discussion, who were in Vietnam as a reporter and a U.S. marine, respectively, spoke of heavy artillery and "serious combat" there. Casualty figures put the killed in action deaths for the entire war at about 58,200 (rounded from 58,178). Also startling is the fact that amputations and crippling lower body injuries were three times more prevalent in Vietnam than WWII.

1969 POLITICS AFFECTING VIETNAM

"Everybody knows that" is a line from a current TV ad that also applies to the statement that Richard Milhous Nixon succeeded Lyndon Baines Johnson as President of the United States in early 1969. Johnson had inherited the conflict in Southeast Asia from his predecessors and he passed it on, having come to believe that Vietnam was "un-winnable" but nevertheless had escalated it. There will be no attempt here to judge the policies of either Johnson or

Nixon, only facts, which could be biased by omission or inclusion. Nixon's campaign pledge of "peace with honor" seemed to be popular as one poll found that in October 71% of Americans approved of his Vietnam policy. Don't get me started on polls, though. Let's just say there are many ways to skew statistics. He sanctioned the secret bombing of Cambodia in March and when news of the bombing hit the newspapers, Nixon ordered FBI wiretaps on four journalists and thirteen government officials to find the leak.

Nixon did propose a peace plan, in May, but Hanoi, N. Vietnam's capital city, rejected it. Around that time, anti-war protests were increasing. A gathering of demonstrators in California claimed they were sprayed with skin-stinging powder by the National Guard to force them to disperse. The previous month, 300 Harvard students, calling themselves Students for a Democratic Society (SDS) took over an administration building and locked themselves in to protest the war.

The Nixon Doctrine, however, was "the U.S. expects Asia allies to take care of their own military defense". He called it "Vietnamization'". He followed with two important actions: First, the withdrawal of the first troops from Vietnam and second, a visit to South Vietnam by the Nixon's. His wife Pat visited wounded soldiers near Saigon and the President shook hands with infantry soldiers to the south. Nixon showed his personable side by asking each soldier about his favorite football or baseball team as he shook each hand. Meeting with Nguyeh Van Thieu was part of the trip, with code name, Moon glow, that was not originally scheduled. He discussed changes in military tactics with both President Thieu and U.S. senior military commanders. It was Nixon's eighth visit to Southeast Asia but his first as President.

When he spoke to the troops, Nixon said some things that seemed right at the time, but in hindsight have been disputed. "This is the most difficult (war) any army has fought… I know that you know why you are here. What happens in Vietnam will determine what happens to peace and freedom in Asia." The problem was that many soldiers didn't know why they were fighting half way across the world for freedom for people that didn't seem to care and protest back home were disheartening. Also, many analysts no longer believe that peace and freedom in Asia were dependent on the outcome in Vietnam.

Hamburger Hill was a pivotal point in opposition to the war. Forty-six men of the 101st Airborne were killed and 400 injured in a fierce ten-day battle to take the hill. Unfortunately after it was taken, the American troops who had fought so hard for it, were told to abandon it. The North Vietnamese moved in and reclaimed it. The wasted lives in that operation caused public outrage back in the U.S. It is also thought that the result for the soldiers in Vietnam was a decline in morale and discipline. Some reports say drug use increased there, but the extent is not documented any more than the actual increase of drug use by college students and protestors is. Anyone who lived in that time can tell you that the use of some drugs did increase, but not specifically when or by how much in 1969.

Another thing that shaped and even changed people's view of Vietnam was the cover of Life Magazine on June 27, 1969. "The Faces of the American Dead in Vietnam" featured photos that broke the collective heart of America. The public outcry was strong for ending the war. Nixon worked with the Joint Chiefs of Staff and formulated a plan for troop redeployment back to America. Originally, 50,000 were to return in July and another 50,000 in September. The actual number of soldiers returning home was a good bit less, but it seemed to be a start.

∞∞

In Paris toward the end of summer, Henry Kissinger met in secret with Xuan Thuy, a representative of North Vietnam. Kissinger proposed mutual withdrawal of troops and warned that U.S. would consider measures of "grave consequence" if no progress was made by November. Xuan Thuy insisted that the U.S. would have to withdraw first and abandon the Thieu government. (South

Vietnam). With the impasse, the two still agreed to keep the channel between them open.

Trying to isolate the 1969 Nixon from his actions in later years seems to result in deeming him as a President who tried to fulfill campaign promises while remaining inscrutable about the war. He did work with the Joint Chiefs of Staff to reduce the number of troops in Vietnam and claimed he had a plan to end the war. But he alternated that with rhetoric about removing government restraints on use of armed forces there. Just as previous administrations failed to commit enough to winning the war, Nixon's efforts weren't substantial enough to satisfy protestors who wanted "peace now". His later mistakes, including the Watergate scandal, are outside the scope of this book. It remains, though, that in 1969, he was confident that he had an approval rating, from the Gallup poll, of at least 60% with the American people and his confidence was high in 1969.

The last quarter of 1969 saw the death of Ho Chi Min, President of the Democratic Republic of Vietnam (North Vietnam), who said in his will that his country should continue to fight on "until the last Yankee has gone." Around that time North Vietnam's Prime Minister, Pham Van Dong "wished success" to American war protestors causing Vice-President Spiro Agnew to call the anti-war groups "communist dupes". One quarter of a million anti-war demonstrators assembled peaceably in Washington, D.C. as part of a moratorium across the U.S. to end the war. There was a strong feeling on the part of many Americans that the anti-war protests were having a negative effect on the fighting soldiers. Many wondered why they were fighting an unsupported war. In November, Nixon asked "the silent majority" to join in solidarity with his Vietnam War effort. His "Vietnamization" plan was to train and equip S. Vietnam to take over the fighting. The plan was popular in the election of Nixon. The European Journal of American Studies documents a Gallup poll where 53% of the general public, in August of 1969, thought the U.S. made a mistake getting involved in Vietnam but many of them supported the "fight or get out" view of the "hawks". Famous hawks, like Shirley Temple Black, thought the U.S. should mine the approaches to the principal port, Haiphong, to cut off supplies from Red China and the Soviets. That was done a few years later. Hawks turned out to vote as backlash against riots, protestors, and the counter-culture. The modern conservative moment had roots in 1969 also. The "rise of the Right" appealed to those who favored limited government, state's rights, lower taxes, and individual freedom and supported the war. The Young Americans for Freedom (YAF) and other Young Republicans groups were active on college campuses also.

By the end of 1969, however, 69% of students identified themselves as "doves" rather than "hawks". Peaceful demonstrations did have an impact on the decision to end the war. But other voters indicated support for a strong military and a renewed cold war when voting. Admiral Thomas Moorer, Chairman of the Joint Chiefs of Staff, advocated an invasion of North Vietnam. Of course, military expenditures, the loss of lives, and lack of success all played a part, too. There was hope that Nixon would not continue the caution Johnson had displayed in regards to the war. Lyndon Johnson's claim that the aim of Vietnam was to secure an independent, non-communist South Vietnam coupled with former Secretary of Defense McNamara's contention that the real goal was not to help an ally, but to "contain China", were cast aside by many Americans who were appalled by the carnage of the war. The fight against communism became secondary to "bringing the boys home". The release of photos of the My Lai massacre didn't help the military's image. Nick Turse, of the Harvard Radcliffe Institute for Advanced study quoted a veteran who said, "A Cobra helicopter gunship, spitting out 600 rounds a minute, doesn't distinguish between chickens, kids, and Viet Cong". The numbers are not exact, but over the course of the war an estimated 2 million Vietnamese civilians were killed. America lost 58,178 men and women.

THE PENTAGON PAPERS

Daniel Ellsberg, a former U.S. Marine officer with a PhD in economics from Harvard secretly photocopied material from the Report of the Office of the Secretary of Defense in 1969. Now known as The Pentagon Papers, the document wasn't leaked to the New York Times until 1971. Classified information about covert involvement with Indochina by the Truman, Eisenhower, Kennedy, and Johnson administrations embarrassed the White House, leading to the Watergate Scandal in 1972. Some writers compare Ellsberg to Snowden (2013).

PRISONER OF WAR

John McCain suffered two broken arms and injured one leg when his plane was shot down during a bombing in Hanoi (North Vietnam) in October of 1967. He was moved to a prison camp and remained in one of several for five and a half years. (One source says Hoa Loa prison known as the "Hanoi Hilton" and another says he was held at a prison known as "The Plantation" and various prison camps.) The future Senator only gave his name, rank, and serial number and was beaten after refusing to sign a statement of disloyalty to the United States. A critic of McCain who claims to have been a POW with McCain says the torture stopped after September 1969 and detainees received better food and health care. However, McCain cannot raise either arm above his shoulders to this day as a result of poor treatment of his broken arms. He received the Silver Star, Bronze Star, Purple Heart, and Distinguished Flying Cross following his release in 1973, two months after the cease fire agreement.

WOMEN IN VIETNAM

The U.S. Government has detailed statistics on the demographics of the men who served from August 5, 1964 to May 7, 1975 such as race, draft status, hostile and non-hostile deaths, and age. (See reference for veteranshour.com in the back of the book). The data on women in Vietnam is not so well documented.

One source claims at least 1200 female soldiers were stationed in Vietnam, mostly in Saigon, Mekong Delta, and the largest army headquarters in the world at that time, Long Binh. The government source says 7,484 women served with 83.5% or 6,250 as nurses. But the many civilians from The Red Cross, USO, Catholic Relief Services, newspapers, and other humanitarian groups are not counted in that number. Of the women from the Women's Army Corps and the Women's Air Force most were clerks but some were physicians, air traffic controllers, and intelligence officers. The foreign correspondent at the Vietnam symposium, Laura Palmer, and two other Vietnam veterans, Camilla Wagner and Jeanne Bell, described the biggest disadvantage to women in Southeast Asian territory; they weren't allowed to carry weapons, even for defense. Camilla, a WAF supply clerk sustained shrapnel to her leg and back when someone threw a grenade at her group as they were leaving their hotel. Jeanne, who was 19 when she served said, "You never know when you're going to get mortared" and had to avoid machine gunfire (essentially hide) because of the no weapons policy. Laura Palmer, reporter at the symposium said because they couldn't take weapons, "survival mode kicked in". Over the course of the war, however, only one woman was killed in action, but many of the nurses had lifelong problems after what they witnessed in evacuation hospitals.

THE NATIONAL GUARD

Not every Army or Air National Guard member served in Vietnam, but many were deployed there in 1969, including Kentucky's 2nd Battalion 138th Artillery, Indiana's Company D (Rangers), Kansas's 69th Infantry Brigade, California's 1st Squadron 18th Armored Cavalry, New Hampshire's 3rd Battalion 198th Artillery, and Hawaii's 29th Infantry Brigade. Members of the Ohio National Guard, the Pennsylvania Air National Guard, and others also served but specific information on 1969 is not readily available. Air Guard units from New York's 156th, Colorado's 120th, New York's 136the, and Iowa's 174th among others flew 24, 124 combat and sortie missions and logged 38,614 flying hours and the fine F-100 Air National Guard squadrons were described as the best in the field.

POINTS TO PONDER

61% of the men killed were 21 years of age or younger

West Virginia had the highest death rate

70% of men sent to Vietnam were lower-middle/working class

10.6% of the soldiers were black accounting for 12.5% of total deaths

3,403,100 personnel served in Laos, Vietnam, Cambodia and other Southeast Asia Theatre locations including fighters in Thailand, sailors in South China Sea Waters; a total of 514,300 offshore workers

82% of veterans who saw heavy combat believe the war was lost because of the lack of political will

75% of the public today agrees with them

COMMENT

Although a majority of Americans were in favor of "bringing the boys home", the actual welcome was often less than glorious. Vietnam veterans were sometimes jeered or worse with no parades or honors such as were present for World War II veterans. In his book, <u>When I Was a Young Man</u>, *Bob Kerrey (later Senator from Nebraska), Navy SEAL, says two things about that. After returning from Vietnam and a Philadelphia hospital where he was fitted with prosthesis on his shattered leg, he remarked, "Though many sought to avoid it, the anti-war movement had became anti-military." Later as he hitchhiked to Lincoln, students coming back from a moratorium stopped to pick him up when they saw his uniform and told him, "We're not against soldiers, just the war."*

In research, I found myself reading more about the Vietnam War than I wanted to include in the book, so I listed some of those sources in the back of the book. They include Kerrey's memoir, a news correspondent's journal and a book compiled from mementos, poems and letters left at the Vietnam War Memorial. I warn you that the last one by Laura Palmer will not be easy to read but it honors those "who are ours" and shouldn't be forgotten. One survivor's journal in it describes 1969 in Vietnam and its unspeakable horrors—unspeakable, too, for many veterans who were unable to talk to anyone about the war, partly because no one wanted to hear about Vietnam. For veterans who survived, it is probably a case of too little too late, but a simple "Thank you for your service", spoken to any 60–70 year old Vietnam veteran you meet, might help.

CHAPTER SIX

HILLARY RODHAM AND COLLEGIATE VIEWS

In the June 20, 1969 issue of Life Magazine, valedictorians that spoke at commencement voiced their concerns and ideas. Hillary Rodham was the first student commencement speaker at Wellesley College. An NBC news article states that Hillary Rodham was not a valedictorian, but was an honor student. The entire text of her speech can be viewed on the Wellesley College Trustees site by typing "Hillary Rodham 1969 speech" in your browser box and selecting the Wellesley site.

Some of her words reflect 1969 views on many campuses around the country.

"The issues of sharing power and responsibility have been general concerns on campuses throughout the world… we are, all of us, exploring a world that none of us understands and attempting to create within that uncertainty. But there are some things we feel—we feel that our prevailing, acquisitive and competitive corporate life, including, tragically, the universities, is not the way of life for us. We're searching for more immediate, ecstatic and penetrating modes of living. And so our questions, our questions about our institutions, about our colleges, about our churches, about our government, continue."

"Every protest, every dissent, is unabashedly an attempt to forge an identity in this particular age."

"There's a very strange conservative strain that goes through a lot of New Left collegiate protests that I find very intriguing because it harks back to a lot of the old virtues, to the fulfillment of original ideas. And it's also a very unique American experience. It's such a great adventure. If the experiment in human living doesn't work in this country, in this age, it's not going to work anywhere."

∞∞

Other top students expressed more radical views. At Brandeis University, Justin D. Simon cautioned that colleges were run by the economic elite of society and suggested that those who supported the Vietnam War should pay for it. The Yale valedictorian felt Yale students were frustrated and despairing about the war. He said, "as long as the fighting continues at its present level, our opposition to the war will also continue." Stephanie Mills of Mills college warned that man has "horribly disfigured this planet, ungrateful and shortsighted animals that we are" and warned of an unrosy future filled with famine and plague. Finally, the valedictorian at Brown University recited a litany of "realities" that he was unwilling to accept, saying, "We should lose sleep" because we are allowing them to go on and accepting them.

Of course some commencement speakers were not students but noteworthy individuals from the government or universities. Here is a line summarizing what three of them said:

Spiro Agnew, Vice President (at Ohio State): "Tomorrow you are the Establishment."

Daniel P. Moynihan, White House Special Advisor (at Notre Dame): "Government can't provide a meaning to life."

Robert F. Goheen, President of Princeton (at Princeton): "You can't afford to be more than 85% right." (If you want to persuade someone to your view)

The inference that students in 1969 were idealistic with a touch of naivety and that their elders took a defensive stance and were "the voice of experience" would not necessarily follow, though. Some institutional leaders sat down and opened dialogues with students and openly protested the war, while others took a strong stand against them. Many young people held conservative views but others may have gone too far with their protests. However, the seeds of social change were placed and nurtured by the thoughts and views of students on college campuses throughout the country even though women's rights and civil rights where not always addressed by these commencement speakers.

It should also be noted that Hillary Rodham wrote her 1969 senior thesis that year but the details are not well documented enough to be included.

CHAPTER SEVEN

THE PEACE MOVEMENT

Although people today may remember the peace movement of 1969 with the slogan "make love, not war", a large number of pacifists had deeply held beliefs, working diligently to not just end the war, but to promote peace everywhere. Not only were there sit-ins and moratoriums by the counter-culture on campuses or in the cities, but also "pray for peace" meetings and services were held by mainstream Americans. Anti-war protestors were not just hippies, drug addicts, or promoters of free love. Many Americans, tired of war, added their voices to protest the Vietnam War. Many high school choirs and choruses at spring concerts performed a song that has become a much-performed lyric.

"LET THERE BE PEACE ON EARTH"

>Let there be peace on earth
>And let it begin with me:
>Let there be peace on earth,
>The peace that was meant to be.
>
>With God as our Father
>Brothers all are we,

Let me walk with my brother
In perfect harmony,

Let peace begin with me,
Let this be the moment now;
With every step I take,
Let this be my solemn vow:
To take each moment and live each moment
in peace eternally.
Let there be peace on earth
And let it begin with me.

*From the song by Jill Jackson and Sy Miller, Copyright 1955, 1983 by Jan-Lee Music, ASCAP. International Copyright secured. All rights reserved.

*Used with permission
The words were felt deeply by everyone who sang them, including me at a 1969 high school concert. It was not hard to project those feelings to the future. The peace movement had it's hangers-on for the music, weed, and free love, but make no mistake there were plenty of people who believed deeply in peace and non-violent life styles. These people were sensitive, hardworking individuals who sacrificed much for the cause of peace. The comment at the chapter end illustrates just how much was sacrificed.

PROTEST

As part of the anti-war movement, some protestors read the names of 33,379 servicemen and women killed in Vietnam to date. On my campus this was a solemn couple of hours. But on May 9, 1969 at the University of Kansas, the reading was the prelude to knocking down the gates to where the Chancellor was to review ROTC candidates. No one was hurt, but it was believed that the Students for a Democratic Society (SDS) were behind it. Infiltrators like the SDS, Weathermen (a revolutionary faction of SDS), other anarchists, and Socialist and Communist recruiters, were a problem at peace rallies, as were others who liked making trouble. As I said above, though, the majority simply wanted the war to be over. Nixon said on December 8, 1969 that the "Vietnam War is coming to a conclusion as a result of the plan that we have instituted. On April 20, 1970 he announced withdrawal of another 150,000 troops within a year.*

COMMENT

*Unfortunately, on April 30, 1970, Nixon announced the incursion into Cambodia inconsistent with ending the Vietnam War. All over the country, campuses erupted in protest over the expansion of the war into Cambodia.

Though the administration of Kent State University had banned a planned peace rally on Monday May 4, 1970, students began gathering for the noon rally. National Guardsmen arrived, armed with rifles and bayonets. The Guardsmen unexpectedly fired and four students were killed with nine others injured. Two of the dead had not participated in the protest at all and one girl, who had grown up a few miles from me, was an honor student. Schools reacted swiftly, with about 400 colleges and universities closing early and sending students home on Credit/No Entry system for work to date. (Personally, the tragedy played a part in my decision to transfer to the University of Pittsburgh near home for my junior and senior years). There is more to the Kent State story and these two sources are recommended:

"The May 4 Shooting at Kent State University: The Search for Historical Accuracy" by Jerry M. Lewis and Thomas R. Hensley, Published by The Ohio Council for the Social Studies Review, Vol 34 Number 1, Summer 1998, pp.-21

"Kent State Shooting", Ohio History Central. www.ohiohistorycentral.org

Jeanie Bryson Clemmens

ACTIVISM IN 1969

In 1969, social groups formed according to shared values, of course. Discarding those that lived in communes and ultra conservative hermits, you would find a group in the middle that was not homogeneous, however. The "student body" of many colleges and universities was like the kitchen sink after busloads of diverse people stopped in to eat.

The forming of Greenpeace in 1969 brought people of many backgrounds to environmental debates. The women's movement crossed over as well, too. The glass ceiling was on the minds of many women who planned to move up in the corporate world. Women who were in "no strings relationships" started to wonder if they were being taken advantage of and struck off on their own. The beginnings of the civil rights protests and the women's movement may not have started in 1969, but they grew and dotted that year with seeds for change.

The assassination of Martin Luther King the previous year shocked young people of black and white color and still had an effect on society in 1969. The youth population, especially, started to break boundaries. To the consternation of both sets of their parents, some young people dated interracially, though it was not really common. Some whites were even "proud" to show off their black friendships and lack of prejudice, but many blacks didn't want that notoriety, preferring to embrace their own culture.

Reverend Jesse Jackson commented "While we can send man to the moon, we can't get foodstuffs across town to starving folk in the teeming ghettos." African Americans lost jobs to white candidates and often made less money. Sadly, most of the handgun deaths were fifteen-to-eighteen year-old black males. Tension between blacks and whites often resulted in shouting matches and even violence. In his book, <u>Decade of Nightmares</u>, Philip Jenkins related, "talk of open race war did not seem fanciful". Because African Americans served alongside whites in Vietnam, many people sympathized with the civil rights movement but also feared mass social conflict.

In order for progress to be made, both sides had to contribute; to stop shouting and work together. The riots of 1967 in Detroit and Newark were over, however, and more attention was paid to reducing poverty and convincing universities to add Black Studies Programs to their curriculum. At Cornell University and North Carolina A & T University at Greensboro, several protests were demands for the hiring of African American faculty as well as for Black Studies programs. An indicator of how slowly change occurred, however, was this: The University of South Carolina Office of Multicultural Student Affairs responded (to the newly-formed Black Studies group's request for a Black Studies Program) by offering a course titled "Negro History". Thirty-eight students completed the class anyway.

An unknown male student leader reportedly told a feminist, "Cool down, little girl. We have more important things to do here than talk about women's problems." However, the FBI thought a lot about the women's movement, viewing it as part of the enemy and a challenge to American values. They even paid informants to infiltrate liberal and radical women's groups. True feminists focused on removing obstacles to legal rights, such as voting and property, and fighting for workplace equality, while extremists took up the fight for reproductive rights and knocking down barriers to "men-only" clubs and sports. However, colleges and universities did respond favorably to some changes. Yale University admitted women in 1969 and became the first all-male Ivy League school to do so but Columbia College remained single sex. Princeton University actually printed two sets of acceptance/rejection letters to women in their first year of admitting women in 1969. Administration expressed the opinion that, "a mixed-sex school improves the learning atmosphere" but they were prepared to reject women if the tide changed. Although inroads were made in the professions, military and media sectors, and prevention of domestic violence, working for Women's Studies programs on college campuses was more successful in promoting understanding.

Colleges and universities were not the only source of activism in 1969, however.

The Girl Scouts changed and, by passing Action 70, the organization made a commitment to racial equality. In 1969 the first African American woman became Vice President of the Girl Scouts of America and many troops became integrated. As a spokesperson for a Skokie, Illinois elementary school said, "since schools are now integrated, then clubs and activities should be also".

CHAPTER EIGHT

A DIFFERENT SORT OF ACTIVISM

While some of the 704,000 females in college in 1969 might be advocating feminism and protesting sexism, there were at least 150,000 women who accomplished a great deal and were a little less vocal.

GENERAL FEDERATION OF WOMEN'S CLUBS

From the 1890's on women all over the country started actively working for the improvement of public education, better child labor laws, and other civic projects in their local chapter of Women's Clubs. In January 1969, the Illinois chapter held a benefit to raise money to purchase a new bus for the American Indian Center when they had to rent one to replace their van that had been vandalized. They did so by shopping at a local "finer foods" store, which donated 5% of sales to the cause. Other clubs held fashion shows or luncheons to help schools, start or preserve public libraries, and improve the juvenile justice system. The exact number of women who were GFWC members is hard to pin down but membership peaked in 1955 at 850,000 and is around 100,000 today.

BUSINESS AND PROFESSIONAL WOMEN'S CLUBS

Founded in Brooklyn in 1908 by Alice Wiley Seay, it is the umbrella group of New York State African American Women's Groups. Their goal, in 1969 as well, was to "uplift work among girls and young women". In the 60's NABPW also organized boys' clubs too. The minutes from their 1969 meetings are missing or not available, as are the group's reactions to the upsurge of African American activities in 1969, but the beauty pageants they sponsored and the girls' clubs they formed had a positive influence on young girls and women of color.

PEO

This low profile group became publicly recognized as a philanthropic educational organization in 2005 but in 1969, the 130,000+ members were quietly going about their business providing scholarships and support to Cottey College (founded by PEO), and helping students through their Educational Loan Fund and the International Peace Scholar Awards.

WHAT ABOUT THE MEN?

Of course over 500,000 were in Vietnam and about 812,000 were in college but many were active in these groups:

ROTARY INTERNATIONAL

With 1.2 million Rotarians in 34, 282 clubs all over the world today, it wouldn't be wrong to assume that there were many Rotarians in 1969. Founded in 1905 they rotated meeting among the offices of each member, hence the name Rotary. With an ongoing commitment to service, Rotary is active in the community and Rotary International joined the fight against polio by helping to immunize 6 million children in the Philippines (1979). They sponsor service clubs for 18–30 year olds, provide resources for future leaders with Rotary Youth leadership Awards, and strive to build goodwill and better friendships. Women are welcome, as Dianne Feinstein, U.S. Senator, is a Rotarian. Others of note are Frank Borman, U.S. Astronaut, Warren G. Harding, President, Marconi, inventor, Sibelius, composer, and Harry Lauder, Scottish entertainer.

LIONS CLUB INTERNATIONAL

Also with current world membership in the millions, Lions clubs are dedicated to community service. Just a few of their goals are "to create and foster a spirit of understanding among peoples of the world", "to promote…good citizenship", and "to encourage service-minded people to serve their community without personal financial reward". Most often this is done through their sight programs and hearing and cancer screening projects. This group was alive and active in 1969 as well.

KNIGHTS OF COLUMBUS

Of course many churches were actively involved in the community besides the Catholic Church, (see below) but the Knights has a membership that exceeds the Lions Club and the Rotary, and they deserve mention here. A few years before 1969, the KOC took steps to counter charges of racial discrimination. In 1969, the order contributed $75,000 to the US Catholic Conference's Task Force on Urban Problems to help address poverty and discrimination. They continue to be a force for public good. An aside, they started the campaign to add "under God" to the Pledge of Allegiance. John F. Kennedy was a Fourth Degree Knight.

CHARITIES

A list of U.S. charitable organizations in 1969 is lengthy so suffice it to say Americans gave over $125 billion (in inflation adjusted dollars) to charitable organizations that year. Causes ranged from medical research to community action.

Total giving from all sources (living individuals, bequests, and foundations) was $1.6 billion in 1969. Parks and other civic projects were the primary beneficiaries of the $47 million left to civic and culture groups. Small drives, like the Harvard Combined Charities drive for everything from black community action to Ethiopian Literacy, hoped to raise $30,000 while The United Way raised $767,000. Catholic Charities in every city and state existed to serve and address the needs of individuals, families, and groups in their community who were vulnerable, especially the poor. In Paterson, New Jersey the director of Catholic Charities expanded programs to include mental health, refugee resettlement, and crisis intervention. The Archdiocese of New York supported the "war on poverty" in what they termed "the turbulent 60's" and opened Covenant House in Manhattan's Lower Eastside to help homeless and runaway youth.

The Protestant and Jewish communities also ministered to those in need in a variety of ways. Jewish Family and Children's Services served the poor and working classes in many ways and later funded day schools. In 1969 they also began outreach programs to help the elderly. Protestant churches continued their good works throughout the year with everything from bake sales, clothing drives, rummage sales, and direct donations to help needy children and families to blood drives, military assistance, and support for the elderly in their communities. Other charities included The Red Cross, United Way, and Armed Forces Charities. In 1969, The Red Cross had over 2.3 million volunteers of which 210,000 or more were connected with fund-raising.

SCIENCE AND RESPONSIBILITY

Two groups that formed in 1969, that were not charities, but represented altruism in science, were The Union of Concerned Scientists and the think-tank, The Hastings Center (August

28, 1969). Students and faculty at M.I.T. founded the Union of Concerned Scientists and The Hasting Center, now in Garrison, New York represented the trend of scientists to take responsibility for the effects of scientific innovation.

VOLUNTEERS

The 1970 Giving USA report lists the volunteer strength of a number of charities ranging from 2,390,00 American Cancer Society volunteers to 208,000 for the YWCA and including twenty other national agencies. Crediting an increase in volunteerism partly to the student volunteer movement, at least 1000 volunteer based programs came from various campuses. In all they reported 1.8 million volunteers for 2,250 campaigns.

The Peace Corps was active in 1969 with 10,500 members serving in 59 countries. Most of the volunteers were college graduates or more with law degrees or MBA's. Volunteers In Service To America (VISTA) volunteers numbered 6,000 in 1969 with 70% of them 24 years old or less. Most of them provided services to poor children in low-income urban areas.

CHAPTER NINE

SLANG, WHO SANG, AND HOPE LANGE

Beach bunnies (non-surfing girls) and ankle-biters (little children) picked up some "off the wall" expressions that surfaced in 1969. If you were "now" (fashionable) "for real" with "killer" looks you were definitely "out of sight" (great). But a "scuzz bucket" who talked "jive" or someone "tagged" as a "square" book buster frequenting "chalk talks" (school lectures) or "strung out" on drugs or grungy, you were "the pits". Here are a few phrases that survived to the present day:

For cars: "wheels" "shotgun" "thumb a ride" "chicken" (race with cars head-on) and "rag top". "Passion pit" for a drive-in movie didn't last because neither did the drive-in theatre.

People who were close were "tight" and a freeloader was a "leaner". Authority figures were known as "the man" or the "heat". Giving off weird "vibes" or being "uptight" was uncool and a "turn off" to people who were "together" and "laid back". Also there was a lot of hanging–"hang a left" (turn left), "hang loose", "hang tough", "hang out", and hang-ups (habits you were stuck on). After a hard day at the beach catching some "rays" some beach bunnies were ready to "sack out" and go to sleep. I think, "meanwhile back at the ranch", which is an expression to remind a speaker to get to the point and off some tangent, is appropriate here. We should move on to entertainment that year.

HIT SONGS

Iron Butterfly's "In-a-gadda-da-vida" was a #1 song of the year but there were still plenty of bubblegum songs, classics, and rock and roll to please everyone. "Sugar, Sugar" by the Archies was Billboard's #1 song in 1969. Radio still plays these Billboard top hits:

Build Me Up Buttercup (Foundations)
Sweet Caroline (Neil Diamond)
Na Na Na Na Kiss Him Goodbye (Steam)
More Today Than Yesterday (Spiral Staircase)
Son of a Preacher-man (Dusty Springfield)
My Way (Frank Sinatra)
Proud Mary (Credence Clearwater Revival)
Something (Beatles)
Sugar Sugar (Archies)

The Grammy's featured other groups in different categories. Country and Western awards went to Tammy Wynette (artist) and "A Boy named Sue" by Shel Silverstein and Johnny Cash as best C & W song. Best blues group was The Isley Brothers and Jazz awards were given to Wes Montgomery and Quincy Jones. Nilsson's rendition of "Everybody's Talking at Me" from "Midnight Cowboy" was the best vocal performance and the group vocal leader was "Aquarius/Let the sun shine in" (Hair) by the Fifth Dimension. Aretha Franklin was top female blues singer and Crosby, Stills, and Nash were highest rated new artists.

To young people today, Bob Dylan is only someone who appeared in the 2014 commercial for Chrysler, but his songs, Blowin in the Wind, The Times They Are A-Changing and many others, including protest songs, were often sung around campfires or at group gatherings in 1969. From The Beatles and The Beach Boys, to Neil Diamond and Elvis Presley, as "far out" as Pink Floyd and Jimi Hendrix, and as tame as Beethoven and Henry Mancini, music was a big influence. However, there was much more. Firesign Theatre was a popular album with the line "How can you be in two places at once when you're not anywhere at all?"

Some musicians, like Henry Mancini found even greater success with popular music. Not only did Mancini produce the Theme from Romeo and Juliet, but also he composed the music for The Pink Panther cartoons. Some fans also liked the deep, rich voice of Jim Nabors, who played the buffoon Gomer Pyle USMC from 1964–1969. The show was a comedy that never mentioned war or Vietnam. His series ended that year but he had a lot of company with the canceling of Peyton Place, The Avengers, Start Trek, The Saint, and Match Game.

NEW TV SHOWS

Most new shows aired in September of 1969, as that was the usual time for new pilots each year. Among the shows to choose from were Laugh-in (most watched), Gunsmoke, Bonanza, Mayberry RFD, Family Affair, Here's Lucy, Marcus Welby M.D., and Walt Disney's Wonderful World of Color. Robert Young and James Brolin won Emmy's for Marcus Welby while Grant Tinker and Norman Lear's Room 222 earned the award with Michael Constantine and Karen Valentine also taking home the prize for that show. So where does Hope Lange come in?

"The Ghost and Mrs. Muir" didn't earn an Emmy itself, but Hope Lange received one for "Continued Performance by an Actress", perhaps because she was the only one who could see and hear the ghost (Edward Mulhare) and had to react and act normally almost simultaneously when both the ghost and other people were present. William Windom (Dr. Seth Hazlett on Murder She Wrote) and his series "My World and Welcome To It" also earned Emmy's that year.

"Scooby Doo, Where Are You?" made an impact on September 13 and although it is one of my favorites, it was overshadowed by the tremendous success of Sesame Street, launched on November 10. While everyone recognized the genius and talent of Jim Henson and Frank Oz in puppeteering and bringing voices to the Muppets, lesser known is the vision of Joan Ganz Cooney and Lloyd Morrisett, who jointly created the TV program as a way to harness the television addiction of children and do something good with it. Learning numbers with The Count (1, ah-ha-ha; 2 ah-ha-ha) and the alphabet with Grover, Kermit, Bert, and Ernie became so popular that Sesame Street was the most watched television program in the world for years. Teachers noticed that children starting school had a greater understanding of letters and numbers than ever before. After Henson's sudden death from toxic shock syndrome, he was one of only three others honored on the Hollywood Walk of Fame as both himself and his character, Kermit The Frog. Walt Disney and Mickey, Mel Blanc and Bugs Bunny, and Mike Myers and Shrek were the other three. Frank Oz went on to do the voice of Yoda in the Star Wars movies, but Sesame Street was maybe his greatest achievement.

MOVIES

Topping the list of popular 1969 movies were "Butch Cassidy and the Sundance Kid", "Easy Rider", "Midnight Cowboy" and "True Grit". Movies, which became cult classics, included "Support Your Local Sheriff", "Bambi Meets Godzilla" and the movie cartoons, "The Ant and The Aardvark", and "The Pink Panther". New musicals were "Hello Dolly" and "Paint Your Wagon".

BOOKS

The anti-war novel, Slaughterhouse Five by Kurt Vonnegut about the 1945 bombing of Dresden was popular in 1969. Others included:

- The Godfather (Puzo)
- The Andromeda Strain (Crichton)

- I Know Why the Caged Bird Sings (Angelou)
- Portnoy's Complaint (Roth) sexual revolution story banned in some countries
- The Big Bounce (Elmore Leonard)
- The Campus Murders (Ellery Queen)

Norman Mailer won the Pulitzer Prize for Non-fiction with Armies of the Night.

Children's books included Sylvester and the Magic Pebble (Steig), Richard Scarry's Best Storybook Ever (Scarry), and The Very Hungry Caterpillar (Carle).

The French Lieutenant's Woman (Fowles) and Love Story (Segal) were top romances.

Bored of the Rings: A Parody of J.R.R. Tolkien's Lord of the Rings was published, written by The Harvard Lampoon.

CHAPTER TEN

WOODSTOCK AND THE BOY SCOUTS

If you're under thirty you probably don't know about Woodstock but young people of every generation tend to flock to locations where "something is going on". That's what happened in Bethel, New York on August 15, 1969 at Max Yasgur's dairy farm. The town of Woodstock, where Bob Dylan lived was 60 miles away but the young founders of this soon-to-be infamous music festival thought the name Woodstock sounded good. Those four men, Michael Lang, John P. Roberts, Joel Rosenman, and Artie Kornfield booked music groups and sold 50,000 tickets at $7-$18 for a one to three day pass, except that almost half a million (400,000) young people showed up before they could set up gates and ticket booths. They were forced to make it a free concert even though they had already shelled out $10,000 for the lease of the farm. Locals, who didn't want hippies in their town, boycotted Max Yasgur's milk and they later sued him for collateral property damage. The founders had 70 lawsuits filed against them and were $ 1 million in debt when the festival was over.

Despite thirty-minute lines for water and hour long waits for the port-a-johns, the crowd remained fairly peaceful as most of the crowd just came for the music. They were treated to the following:

- Richie Haves–"Freedom" sometimes referred to as "Motherless Child"

- Ravi Shankar–who played sitar through the rain
- Arlo Guthrie, Joan Baez, and Country Joe MacDonald
- Santana–"Evil Ways"
- Canned Heat–"Going up the Country"
- Grateful Dead–amp blew during "Turn on Your Love Light"
- Creedence Clearwater Revival–"Bad Moon Rising" and "Proud Mary"
- Janis Joplin "Piece of My Heart"
- Sly and the Family Stone–"Everyday People" "Stand" "Dance to the Music"
- The Who–"Pinball Wizard" "See Me, Feel Me"
- Jefferson Airplane–"White Rabbit" and "Somebody to Love"
- Joe Cocker and The Grease Band–"With a Little Help from My Friends"
- Blood Sweat and Tears–"You've Made Me So Very Happy" and more
- Crosby Stills Nash (and Young)–"Judy Blue Eyes" "Marrakash Express"
- Sha-na-na–"Get a job" "At the Hop" "Duke of Earl" "Teen Angel"
- Jimi Hendrix–last to perform–"Purple Haze" "Star-Spangled Banner"

The potential for disaster was great with wall-to-wall-people, rain, thunderstorms during performances on a tall, lightning rod stage with scads of electrical equipment, and a lack of security. It's a wonder that only 40,000 injuries; adverse reactions to drugs, and illnesses, were reported. Donny York of Sha-na-na remembers it on Woodstock.com in August 2014, as "cheerful human warmth, individuals taking good care of each other, sharing resources". But lawsuits and others, who condemned the festival as love without rules that didn't do anything to stop the Vietnam War, suggest otherwise.

The festival ended Monday, August 18, and on Tuesday some of the performers appeared on The Dick Cavett Show. Grace Slick of Jefferson Airplane kept calling Cavett "Jim", and it was the first time the f-bomb was uttered on live TV (not necessarily by Miss Slick). Joni Mitchell, Stephen Stills and Jefferson Airplane performed and the audience got up and danced to "Somebody to Love". Jimi Hendrix appeared with Cavett three weeks later and Dick remarked that Hendrix's style was "unorthodox". "No", replied Hendrix, "it's beautiful" which triggered applause and Cavett blushed. Woodstock launched or elevated the careers of many musicians whose music is still played on the radio. Musically, it was a success, but there are many who say that the whole thing was a disaster of drugs, lack of inhibitions, and amorality. Marijuana was readily available and there was a risk in drinking anything anyone offered as it might contain LSD, mescaline, or Quaaludes. The story of two attendees, who refused all drugs at the concert and just enjoyed the music, can be found at www.ydr.com/ci 13080883, written by Melissa Nan Burke. These two young men were not the typical peace and love hippies that comprised most of the audience. However, the fact that they had been boy scouts leads into another festival on the other side of the country.

THE BOY SCOUT JAMBOREE

The dates of the annual gathering of Boy Scouts coincided with the Moon Landing; July 17–22 1969, therefore the group of 34,251 at Farragut State Park, Idaho watched a delayed broadcast of Neil Armstrong's walk during their evening arena time. The astronaut gave a shout out to "the Scouts at Jambo" from the moon. Along with charcoal stoves, thousands of tents, and "Keep America Beautiful" trash boxes, the scouts had a scale model of the Saturn V rocket in the center of camp. Time was spent patch-trading, participating in a skill-o-rama, cooking and eating.

The contrast between The Boy Scout festival and Woodstock is extreme, of course. An able statistician would throw out the extremes and look at the average or normal groups. Still Earth Day, planned for 1970 helped bring young people from all backgrounds to join in caring for the planet. Many 4H clubs still flourished "to make the best better". (By the way some people who were 4H members are Julia Roberts, Jackie Kennedy Onassis, Archie Manning, Faith Hill, and Johnny Cash.)

Drugs were becoming more prevalent in 1969 but at the time only 12% favored legalizing marijuana as opposed to 58% in 2013. Sociologists would probably agree that, as a whole, young people in 1969, approximately 17–24 year olds were not a homogeneous group as growth and change affected individuals everyday. And young people were not the only age group experiencing lifestyle change.

CHAPTER ELEVEN

OLDER AMERICANS

What was the over 65 crowd doing in 1969? A few retired to Florida, many struggled to live independently on reduced income, and some lived long enough to "become a burden to their children". Those who couldn't live alone were in "convalescent homes" or nursing homes. Retirement villages and assisted living facilities were rare in 1969. President Nixon, however, issued Proclamation 3899 on March 17, 1969 declaring May 1969 as Senior Citizens Month. One goal was to focus on accident prevention and safety for older Americans. 18,899,000 people were 65 and older that year and one fourth of them had incomes below the poverty threshold. 74.7% received Social Security and 9.2% lived on Welfare. The average life expectancy was 70.5 but the elderly were more likely to be widowed and less educated than now (2016). Only 13 % had some college and many had not finished high school. About 815,000 seniors lived in one of 18,000 nursing facilities where 65% were over 65 and of them 32% over 85 and only 12% over 90 years of age. Medicare or Medicaid paid the monthly charges of $328 on average, but up to $800 per month in some cases. Many other older Americans remained independent, however.

Here is a sampling of what some seniors were doing that made them Chicago Hall of Fame selections:

- Woman, 68, a retired caterer, teaches millinery classes
- A male, retired postal clerk, who coaches girls' softball and helps rehabilitate alcoholics
- Woman, 79, attended evening classes to earn GED so she could tutor children
- 62 year old musician and missionary nominated by Martin Luther King Urban Progress Center for volunteer music teaching in hospitals and convalescent homes
- Retired accountant, 86, elected "king" at a senior camp, plays piano for groups
- Former physician/surgeon provides equipment for a camp each year

At Chicago Fair's Golden Age Day, 65 to 90 year olds sang, danced, recited poetry, and displayed homemade jewelry and crafts. They formed a "kitchen band" out of washbasins and honored the oldest woman (98) and man (94). The man, Carlyle Hall won five years straight and said proper diet and exercise was his secret. One woman wore a huge hat with a miniature lunar module and figures planting the flag on the moon.

In a year of mini-skirts, rock music festivals, and "consciousness-raising" the emphasis was on the young and old people were left with the choice of being forgotten and unproductive or making some changes and getting noticed themselves. It wasn't until 1970 that Maggie Kuhn founded The Gray Panthers in response to forced retirement, but the seeds of change were germinating in 1969.

CHAPTER TWELVE

TAKE US TO CUBA?

Do you hate taking off your shoes at airport security? You might be more tolerant if you knew the result of lack of tight security in 1969. A surprising number of hijackings occurred in airports all over the country. Thirty-four planes were diverted, mostly successfully, to Cuba from a number of U.S. airports. In addition to eight from New York and seven from Florida (Miami and Jacksonville), planes from Pittsburgh, Charleston, LA, Dallas, Atlanta were successfully flown to Cuba when the hijackers made demands. An attempted hijacking from Philadelphia was stopped.

The hijackers themselves were a diverse group and included:

Seven Cubans

Nine people later found to be insane

Two American students and one 19-year-old Navy deserter who didn't want to go to Vietnam"

Black Panther, Tony Bryant who later wrote a book "Hijack"

Members of the Quebec Liberation Front

A man "tired of TV dinners and seeing people starve in the world"

If there is humor to be found, though, there is this: Allen Funt, host of TV's "Candid Camera", his wife, and two youngest children boarded an Eastern flight to Miami from Newark. When a hijacker, with a knife, ordered the pilot to divert to Cuba, four passengers (who had spotted Funt) thought it was a stunt. "Candid Camera" shows pulled pranks on people and then Funt revealed himself saying, "You're on 'Candid Camera'". Eventually, the passengers realized it was no prank. The many hours they all spent in Cuba, incommunicado and worried, convinced them.

The plane that was most targeted was the DC-8, but several 727 and 707 models were also hijacked. Among the 114 passengers on Delta Air Lines flight 821, a DC-8 from Dallas, Texas, were 26 Marine recruits headed to San Diego. Luis Antonio Frese, who remained in Havana and was never prosecuted, before it diverted to Miami and it's planned route, hijacked the plane to Cuba.

It is probable that increased airline security could have prevented many 1969 hijackings and lessened overall anxiety about travel that year.

CHAPTER THIRTEEN

THE OTHER OUTER SPACE

There were a few people in 1969 who believed the Moon Landing was faked and that belief still exists today but only with a few. The possibility of life on other planets, however, was as fascinating back then as it is today. UFO's may be easily explained but reports of them were common in 1969. Before I list some of the other 1969 sightings here is a famous one.

Future Governor of Georgia and President of the United States, Jimmy Carter, reported seeing a luminous, not solid, red and green orb radiating in the western sky on January 6, 1969. He was standing outside the Lion's Club in Leary, GA with ten or more other witnesses. He spoke of it later as spectacular and even said, "I am convinced that UFO's exist because I have seen one". His report to the International UFO Bureau was not filed until 1973 and you can view the original handwritten document on the Internet. One well-known UFO skeptic tried to convince people that what Carter saw was Venus, but Venus was in the Southwestern sky on that date, not the west. Also Jimmy Carter was a trained observer having logged many hours on watch in the Navy. He has never backed off the story or conceded it might be some misidentification of natural phenomena.

What follows is not a complete list nor does it provide real evidence of UFO's or prove the reliability of witnesses. As a true fact, in the Condon Report of 1968, Professor Condon states that "witnesses should be examined for defective vision" and cited "fuzzy images" and vague accounts as a reason to say "no further investigations are justified". Here are some (US only) of the UFO sightings in 1969:

Crittendon, VA–Amber lights, one blinking in an elliptical pattern reported on January 17.

Plattville, IL–at 12:30 a.m. a couple driving home described a giant "ice cream cone" shaped object traveling round end first until it halted over their landlord's house. It was 2–3 stories high. Suddenly the car engine died and the lights in it and the surrounding farm security lights went out and the front end of the car began to rise. The wife (driver) screamed and shouted, waking her husband who had been asleep in the front seat. They were able to re-start the car and leave. January 25

Elmer, MO–6:40 a.m., a postal carrier spotted a reddish object .5 miles to his right and about 50 feet above him. It emitted a beam onto the road in front of him and the truck engine stalled and the radio quit. The object changed color, cruised, and then left. March 4

Lancaster, MD–Witness described a domed disc overhead. The car slowed and the dog reacted. The witness reported eye irritation. March 6

Westhope, ND–A disc with a dome shined a light beam illuminating a police chief's car and then flew south. March 10

Lake Havasu, AZ–Cessna 150 encountered fifteen to twenty oval objects in the sky. March 17

Hill City, KS–Multi-colored object came within 100 feet of a witness and hovered. April 14

Silver Spring, MD–Dogs, cats, and horses reacted to a UFO April 23

St. Louis, MO–Passengers and pilots on three airlines (American 112, United, and a National Guard jet) saw four dart shaped objects at 4:00 p.m. FAA radar St. Louis confirmed the formation but was unexplained. June 5

Van Horne, IA–At 11:00 P.M. two young women on a sleepover felt vibrations and heard the windows rattling. They looked out and saw a gray metallic disc with orange/red band of lights around the circumference. It rotated counterclockwise as it rose and sailed away. The parents heard nothing but the girl's father investigated the field location the next day and found a perfect circle with plants wilted as if exposed to intense heat. (Crop circle). Investigators found no motivation or desire for publicity from the witnesses and found corroboration at the tract site. June 13

Outer Space–Apollo 11 astronaut Buzz Aldrin reported a UFO, which experts believe was a piece of Mylar covering blown of the Lunar Module when the attitude rockets were fired repeatedly. July 18

Raleigh, NC–A shiny object approached a car and hovered August 5

Stover, MO–A flock of turkeys reacted to an orange/red disc in the sky. August 31

Glenwood, MO–A dog in a car became agitated when a domed disc appeared above the car. October 10

Of the 146 UFO reports the Air Force received in 1969, only one was classified as unidentified. Project Blue Book, which was the Air Force UFO investigation name, was terminated, or rather Robert Seamans, Secretary of the Air Force announced the termination of Air Force investigations on December 17, 1969. The Air Force position was that they were trained observers who couldn't be fooled. Most scientists didn't want to be in the company of "pseudo scientists, commercial cultists, pulp booksellers, and crackpots" by endorsing the possible existence of UFO's. However, on December 27 at its annual meeting in Boston, the American Association for the Advancement of Science held a panel discussion on UFO's and asked for preservation of the Air Force files for future study. The National Investigating Committee on Aerial Phenomena (NICAP), an independent research group continued their interest and research into UFO's also.

SOVIET SPACE PROGRAM

The Soviet Union, who had beaten the U.S. to launching the first man in space, had more than a few projects that year as well. The Russians concentrated on Venus and sent Venera 5 toward the planet on January 5. The next week Venera 6 was launched, but four days later Soyuz 4 trumped that with a crew. The next day Soyuz 5 was put into orbit to dock with Soyuz 4. The transfer of crews between the two crafts in space was a momentous accomplishment for the Russians. We launched Apollo 9 in March, Apollo 10 in May, and Apollo 11 in July. Pictures of our national triumph on the Moon were featured on the cover of Life Magazine on August 8.

The Russian space program was originally designed to be a military one, focusing on the development of missiles, but priorities changed. In 2014, the competition between the United States and the Soviet Union has become a co-operative effort. Congress passed a resolution granting NASA permission to buy seats on Soyuz to the International Space Station. The U.S. is also dependent on Russia for rocket engines used in Atlas V and Taurus II launch vehicles and Russia needs U.S. funds to help their budget for space ventures. Russia's Star City launch facility is predicted to be the only place to send astronauts from any nation to the International Space Station.

REGULATING OUTER SPACE

Fortunately the United Nations Committee on Peaceful Use of Outer Space (COPUOS) was formed in 1957 to encourage research and dissemination of information on outer space matters. They also study legal problems arising from the exploration of space and oversee astronaut rescue agreements, liability problems, and the outer space treaty. The committee keeps track of the distribution of program-carrying signals by satellites and watches for violations of the treaty banning nuclear weapons tests in space. Anti-satellite rockets such as those launched by The Russian Federation (toward one of their old satellites) are thought to be a violation of "no weapons in space". Recently one of these missiles hit a U.S. satellite designated for Ukraine communications but Russia called it an accident. Does this new flexing of muscles by the Russian Federation and their current show of strength in the Ukraine have grave consequences for world peace? The United States must decide whether to become involved or ignore these aggressive actions. Remember that the U.S. is dependent on rides from Russia to the space station. Can we afford to lose that benefit?

The Russian people had both pride and cynicism about their space program. You could say that about Americans as well. Saying "the Americans are doing such and such in their space program" usually brings an influx of money to the Russian program. They don't want to be outdone. The competition between the two countries has not completely gone away for either country. Americans don't want to lag behind the Russians in anything either, but they're not always willing to support candidates that want to increase space program expenditures. Many Russians, and Americans as well, feel the money budgeted for space could be better spent elsewhere.

The CEO of Amazon.com, Jeff Bezos, has a connection to the 1969 moon landing although he was only five at the time. He led an expedition to find and recover Apollo 11 engines and on March 12, 2012 an engine part was salvaged from the ocean. Examination by experts confirmed that it was part of the Saturn V engine used in the mission. Bezos is more than an aerospace buff. In 2015, his aerospace development and manufacturing company, Blue Origin, launched a rocket into sub-orbit. The company has plans for commercial human spaceflight in the future.

CHAPTER FOURTEEN

1969 COMPANIES

Familiar names of established companies top the list of Fortune 500's 100 picks in 1969: General Motors, Exxon, Ford, General Electric, Chrysler, IBM, Mobil, Texaco, Gulf Oil, and US Steel. Other large companies, not in the top ten, included AT&T, often referred to as Ma Bell in the 60's, (12th), General Foods (44th), Coca-Cola (77th), and Weyerhaeuser (98th). Weyerhaeuser Real Estate was an offshoot that was founded in 1969.

Several companies established in that year: The Janus Capital Group, Sysco, Storage Technology Corporation, and CompuServe, providing investors, the food industry and the computer industry with marketable items. Families gained new dining and shopping choices with the launching of Red Robin, O'Charley's, The Ground Round, The Children's Place, The Gap, Jimmy Dean, and KinderCare Learning Centers. Judi Sheppard Missett, a professional jazz dancer started her dance fitness business, Jazzercise, which grew to 5000 worldwide franchises by 1995. Finally, showing the diversity of culture (and readers) in 1969, two publishing companies were founded: Howard Books, a Christian publishing company in Louisiana, and Shambhala Publications, founded at Berkeley and later moved to Boulder, Colorado. The latter focuses on books with an "enlightened" approach such as eastern religion (Buddhism) and philosophy.

IBM

Today IBM has WATSON, the computer that won on Jeopardy, SPSS Analytical software, and 6,809 patents. You have to go back in the company's history to understand how it grew to the multinational giant it is today. About 100 years ago, The Computing Tabulating Recording Company named Thomas J. Watson, Sr. as CEO. In 1924 he changed the name to International Business Machines and IBM was off to the races. Inventions like the magnetic disk drive, DRAm or RAM, Fortran, and the IBM 701 propelled the company to prominence in the computing world. An IBM 701 rented for $15,000 a month and the 19 total that were manufactured went to atomic research labs (3), aircraft companies (8), government agencies and the Navy, (4), other labs (3), and the U.S. Weather Bureau (1). The faster magnetic core memory, which replaced drum storage, developed by IBM in 1956 brought about the IBM 7090, the fastest computer in the world, at the time. But IBM developers weren't done.

The first of three major events in 1969 was the introduction of magnetic stripe cards, now called credit cards with magnetic strips. Today's thriving credit card industry was jumpstarted.

The second event may have slowed the progress of the company, though. The Justice Department had issued a consent decree in 1956 against IBM requiring the company to sell as well as lease computers and to service and sell parts for IBM computers, even if they no longer owned them. In spite of compliance, U.S. District Court filed suit on January 17, 1969 and *United States vs. IBM* dragged on for 13 years from then. Later, also in 1969, IBM decided to price its software and services separately from the hardware sales, a pivotal moment in computer history. This "unbundling" started the rise of the multi-billion dollar software and service industry. Although the government still claimed that IBM violated the Sherman Antitrust Act by "monopolizing the general purpose electronic digital computer system market, specifically computers designed for business", the suit was found "without merit" in 1981. IBM researchers could now devote time to developing what has become commonplace–the personal computer.

The third significant event involved the Moon Landing in July of 1969. IBM personal computers assisted in the endeavor and IBM personnel worked closely with NASA from then on. It's noteworthy that IBM had been a NASA contractor since 1950.

The next chapter describes the early Internet without much mention of IBM. However, the IBM 360 at the University of California, Santa Barbara was one of the first four in the ARPA Network.

CHAPTER FIFTEEN

ARPANET

For those born after 1960, it might seem ludicrous that Boomers ever stood in line with their stack of keypunched cards to hand to another student to run through the school's mainframe computer. They had to wait hours (a day sometimes) to pick up their green-and-white-striped computer printout to see if their program ran or had error messages. Here is a bit of 1969 computer history that predates even that.

In 1969, the Telstar satellite had been orbiting since 1965, GPS was offered for commercial use, microprocessors existed but weren't readily available, and Bob Propst had "invented" the office cubicle the previous year. Future households (1970's) might have Sinclair, Tandy, Radio Shack or Commodore home computers, but nothing like that was around in 1969. Large, powerful computers that were capable of doing research were few and far between. Within the Department of Defense, ARPA (Advanced Research Projects Agency), the story of the Internet begins.

An ARPA worker, Robert Taylor, had three computer terminals, which ARPA funded, in his office. Their "owners" were identified as System Development Corporation in Santa Monica, Project Genie at University of California, Berkeley, and Multies at M.I.T. There were different user commands for each and if he was logged in and talking to one of them, he had to physically go and log into another to talk to it. He thought, "There ought to be one terminal that goes anywhere you want to go." That idea also occurred to Charles M. Herzfeld, ARPA director from 1965–67. He remarked that while ARPA was usually known for top secret systems and weapons in the Cold War, the real goal now was to allow researchers access to the research computers that were geographically separated from them. There were four such powerful computers at UCLA, Stanford, U.C. Santa Barbara, and University of Utah. Since the computers couldn't be moved to accommodate many researchers across the country, a way was needed to "move Mohammed to the mountain" with remote access.

BBN Technologies was awarded a contract to build a direct multiplex control with a set of 24 indicator lamps showing the status of the Interface Message Processors (IMP). They used a version of the Honeywell DDP-516 computer and each IMP could support up to four hosts. With the addition of packet switching (routers) pioneered by Paul Baran, everything was ready to test.

Someday a Jeopardy question will ask, "What was the first word on the internet?" The judges will have to decide if the first message between UCLA's SDS Sigma computer and Stanford Research Institute's SDS-940 on the ARPANET is the answer. Most historians accept the word "lo" to be the first transmitted word.

At 10:30 p.m. on October 29, 1969 Professor Leonard Kleinrock instructed his programming student, Charley Kline to send an "l" from their UCLA computer that was received by Bill Duvall at Stanford. Then they sent an "o", intending to spell "login". The "o" was received, but Stanford's computer crashed before the "g" making "lo" the first word transmitted on the Internet. If Alex Trebek says, "the first internet words were sent from here, you could answer "Boelter Hall, UCLA."

From that brief success sprang many new firsts. The first permanent ARPANET link was established on November 21, 1969. E-mail was two years away but CompuServe introduced the first commercial online service using the link.

Just like the space program, there were a few failures. Honeywell introduced the "Kitchen Computer" in 1969. It was to be a luxury gift item, but no units were ever sold.

The ARPANET project jump-started the progression from a few computer terminals, linked together by a local connection, to many computers linked to each other, regardless of proximity. Their highly significant success was the seed from which the Internet grew to its current undisputed importance.

CHAPTER SIXTEEN

VITAL STATISTICS

Jennifer Aniston and J-Lo were born in 1969, as were Matthew Perry, Jack Black and Catherine Zeta-Jones. They had no foreknowledge of their future stardom just like Donnie Wahlberg and Danny Wood, who became part of The New Kids on the Block. Sports figures Ken Griffey, Jr (baseball), Kerry Earnhardt (racing) and Chuck Liddel (martial arts) entered the world along with Steffi Graf (tennis) and Angel Cabrera (golf).

As their lives began, others passed away. Dwight D. Eisenhower, Ho Chi Minh, and Joe Kennedy died. Star Judy Garland died of a drug overdose at age 47 and Sharon Tate (actress in Valley of the Dolls) and Leno and Rosemary La Bianca were killed by the Manson cult. Ted Kennedy was driving the car which went into the tidal channel at Chappaquiddick, killing Mary Jo Kopechne, 28, but he was only charged with failing to report the accident until nine hours later. Rocky Marciano, the heavyweight champ, was killed in a plane crash. Other notable deaths were Boris Karloff, of horror movies, and the recipient of the 1st artificial heart.

A frequent guest on the Tonight Show starring Johnny Carson, Tiny Tim tied the knot with Miss Vicky, (Victoria May Budinger). It is difficult to understand why the strangely dressed long-haired Tiny Tim, who used a tiny ukulele to accompany his falsetto singing of "Tiptoe through the Tulips" was so popular, but millions tuned in to view his marriage on the show. Clean cut "Sound of Music" star, Julie Andrews married Pink Panther director, Blake Edwards that year also.

Where there is marriage, divorce is also found. The split between Eddie Fisher (m. Elizabeth Taylor previously) and Connie Stevens was prominent. In sports, Floyd Patterson's wife Sandra Hicks wanted him to quit boxing. When he refused, she divorced him. Star Trek's William Shatner divorced Gloria Rand early in 1969. Bruce Dern and Diane Ladd as well as Woody Allen and Louise Lasser divorced. Other notable divorced couples were Geraldo Rivera (Linda Coblentz) and Ray Kroc of McDonald's (Jane Dobbins).

The passing of the No-Fault-Divorce Law in California with equal division of community property in that year no doubt prompted more divorces in Hollywood in 1969.

CHAPTER SEVENTEEN

TV, TOYS, AND TALK SHOWS (WITH COMMERCIALS, OF COURSE)

"Laugh-in" with Dan Rowan and Dick Martin led the list of most popular shows in 1969 with the "Sock-it-to-Me" girl, Judy Carne and "little old man" Arte Johnson, but surprising the next most watched were westerns, Gunsmoke (James Arness) and Bonanza (Lorne Green). Mayberry RFD with Andy Griffith and Family Affair (Brian Keith) round out the top five with wholesome winning 4-1. A complete list of 1969 TV shows can be found easily on the Internet but highlights include the debut of Sesame Street, Scooby Doo, and The Brady Bunch and the canceling of Star Trek (went to syndication), the Avengers (UK) and The Smothers Brothers Comedy Hour. Tom and Dick Smothers were often politically incorrect and controversial, which could have landed them on Nixon's enemies list (but didn't). Dan Rowan, on the other hand was a Nixon supporter.

Medicals shows like Marcus Welby M.D. starring Emmy Award winner Robert Young and Medical Center succeeded without the graphic displays and gore of modern medical shows. Welby examined fully clothed patients and characters on Medical Center were seen in a sheet up to the neck with a masked doctor hovering. In the next scene the patient was back in the hospital bed, awake.

"Doctor Who" was around in 1969 (UK) and in June 1969 Patrick Troughton made his last appearance as Second Doctor in Episode 10. Jeopardy, Meet the Press, and The Wonderful World of Disney continued that year. Variety shows hosted by Doris Day, Dean Martin, Carol Burnett, and others aired for an hour each. Hee Haw, Here's Lucy (Ball), and the Beverly Hillbillies provided comedy for some viewers.

Commercials for Maxim freeze-dried coffee, Tupperware, Goodyear, and Crackerjack often aired after ten minutes of show time. Many will remember a Clio winner: Dial Soap—"Aren't you glad you use Dial? Don't you wish everybody did?"

TOYS

Toys have been found in civilizations over 4000 years old not only in the Indus Valley in Pakistan but in Meso–America, Greece, and China. While play is not new, ideas about what it is have evolved from just something children do, to a belief that play is essential to development and education. Philosophers Schiller and Spencer proposed that play is "surplus energy" and takes the form of "imitation of a serious activity". Education advocates John Dewey and Maria Montessori suggested that play and work together made a better classroom environment. So what did 1969 parents do when their child answers their request that he or she "go play" with "but I have nothing to play with"? Many made a trip to the store for the latest or most educational toy they could find; however, responding, "What is the matter with all the toys you got for your birthday (or Christmas or Hanukkah)?" was common, too. So what toys were popular in 1969?

- Nerf ball by Parker Brothers–sold 4 million in 1969
- Barbie–these dolls were popular from 1950 on. The National Museum of Play breaks down their doll collections as 1) Barbie and 2) dolls after 1950 (excluding Barbie)

- Anything relating to the Moon Landing: Saturn V rockets, command modules, escape tower–the Saturn V plus base with decals sold for $10.49
- Dancerina Doll–with battery and knob you turned in her back to direct her steps–also included was her own 33 1/3 rpm record all for $17.99
- Junior chemistry set–$24.99
- Double bake oven included 15 cake and icing mixes plus cookie cutters, muffin tins and rolling pin.
- Doctor and nurse kits at $4.99 each
- Hot wheels and matchbox cars
- Beatles Yellow Submarine (England) for $3.99
- Zig-Zag sewing machine $24.99
- Chitty Chitty Bang Bang Model
- NFL magnetic board–electric football
- Lite brite
- Fisher Price Little People
- GI Joe
- Ping pong tables (from $39.95) and train sets (from $9.97)

Some books and cartoons were also considered playthings and Nancy Drew, The Hardy Boys and Peanuts (Charles Schultz) were popular as well. Of course some children had none of these playthings as the 12.1% poverty rate suggests.[1] But at the end of 1969, 96% of households had at least one television set (31.9% owned color TV) and at the end of the day after the kids were in bed, and toys put away, parents joined millions of other adults in turning them on to view late night talk shows.

TALK SHOWS

The Tonight Show starring Johnny Carson was by far the most popular starting at 11:15 EST and running 105 minutes. No one wanted to miss the monologue where Carson poked fun at human nature and events with a delivery that let Americans know it was all right to laugh at themselves. Some of his remarks were taken literally, though, as when he casually mentioned toilet paper hoarding and thousands of people stocked up the next day. His Carson Art Players did parodies of shows and commercials such as Carson rising up from a casket to say, "My broker is E.F. Hutton" and mimicking Karl Malden in an American Express commercial. The show always featured interesting guests; the famous whose careers were made by their appearance–Joan Rivers, Roseanne Barr, Eddie Murphy, Jerry Seinfeld, David Letterman, and Drew Carey and the beloved amateurs such as Jim Fowler, an animal expert who bought a marmoset on the set and it relieved himself on Carson's head. Johnny Carson was a good sport about it always knowing what would get a laugh.

Less remembered are The Mike Douglas Show (afternoon), The Joey Bishop Show, and The Della Reese Show. Ms. Reese's show was the first by an African American woman, but it only lasted a year. News shows that year included Face the Nation, Meet the Press, and the CBS Evening News.

Super Bowl commercials had a smaller audience and of course were less expensive than they are today but advertisers in 1969 included Gillette, RCA color, Right Guard, Schlitz (2), and eight cigarette ads (including discontinued Tareyton with black-eyed users who would rather fight than switch and Silva-thins).

1 Though one source put the poverty rate at 14% in 1969, both econlib.org and fas.org's congressional research service cite 12.1%. Details of reference are in the back of the book.

CHAPTER EIGHTEEN

POVERTY WINS?

Former President Lyndon B. Johnson started the ball rolling with his "War on Poverty" which aimed to not only cure poverty, but to prevent it with The Economic Opportunity Act. In 1964 the poverty rate was 19% and by 1969 it had fallen to 12.1% overall. But the rate among African Americans was 32.2% in 1969. Federal spending on welfare was consistent in the late '60's but didn't include amounts spent on Social Security and Medicare and the Johnson Administration spent $15 million on welfare alone.

When Richard M. Nixon became President, he continued the fight by proposing the Family Assistance Plan with the Economic Opportunity Act on August 8, 1969. Needy families with children would receive $1,600 per year and, as an incentive to work, could keep up to $4,000 in earned income. It was not popular with anyone. Liberals thought the support level was too low and the work requirement seemed like a punishment. Conservatives didn't want any expansion of the welfare bureaucracy or public assistance. Labor unions saw a threat to minimum wage and government caseworkers feared job loss.

Nixon, poor as a child, continued to push his plan because he thought the welfare bureaucracy was inefficient and control by states and municipalities was needed to help the poor. The proposal died in Congress several years later.

In a 2015 New York Book Review article, Christopher Jencks wrote, "The War on Poverty: Was it Lost?" Former President Ronald Reagan thought so, when he said in1988, "We fought the War on Poverty–Poverty Won". Since 1969, the percentage of poor Americans has not jumped drastically, but has steadily increased. Some analysts say this is due mainly to non-work and having children outside of marriage. Others argue an influx of Hispanics contributed. Overall the poverty rate has remained relatively constant since 1969 but some demographics and bureaus have changed.

In 1969, 45.9% of poor Americans lived in the South. There is no data on Hispanics until 1972. The number of domestic social programs in 1969 was 435, contrasted with only 45 in the Eisenhower years.

SCHOOL LUNCHES

President Richard Nixon proclaimed the week starting the second Sunday in October, National School Lunch Week. Apparently, John F. Kennedy started NSLW and every President since then makes it a proclamation. The government would provide free or reduced price lunches with the Department of Agriculture supplying assistance for schools without cafeterias. Technically those students could go home for lunch but the ability of ghetto households to provide adequate nutrition was questionable. Under the Child Nutrition Act, over 19 million children were served. The Summer Food Service Program provided meals when school was not in session. Ninety-nine thousand participated at 1200 schools in the summer. The Black Panther organization served free full breakfasts to schoolchildren in 1969 as well.

CHAPTER NINETEEN

RIVER FIRE, OIL SPILL, AND OTHER HAPPENINGS

On the Cuyahoga River, Cleveland, near the Republic Steel Mill, an oil slick caught fire on an early Sunday morning June 22, 1969. Supposedly, a passing train caused a sparks to ignite pieces of oil soaked debris. The fire caused $50,000 damage to a railroad bridge and Cleveland residents later passed a $100 million bond initiative to fund the Cuyahoga cleanup. Mayor Carl Stokes became deeply involved in urging Congress to become involved in pollution control, which led to the Clean Water Act of 1972. An interesting sidebar is that a much-publicized picture of the fire was actually taken at a more serious river fire in 1952.

80,000 to 100,000 barrels of oil spilled into the channel at Santa Barbara California when Union Oil's offshore platform had a blowout on January 28, 1969. It remains the third largest oil spill right after the Exxon Valdez and the 2010 oil spills. The sludge covered 800 square miles of ocean and 35 miles of coastline. Public outcry and the cost of cleanup led to the National Environmental Policy Act of 1969.

An explosion on the USS Enterprise killed 27 and injured 314 on January 14, 1969 at 8:19 a.m. The crew of 4600 was scheduled for deployment to Vietnam. The cause was a mini MK-32 rocket, loaded on a F-4 Phantom jet, overheated due to exhaust from another vehicle. Fifteen out of the thirty-two aircraft aboard were destroyed in the fire.

An underground nuclear test was conducted at Amchitka Island on October 2, 1969. Project Milrow, as it was called, was supposed to test an island, not a weapon, to produce data, which could predict the impact of large explosions. Shockwaves reached the surface with an acceleration of over 35 g causing a dome 3 kilometers (two miles) in radius to rise five meters (sixteen feet). The explosion turned the surrounding sea to froth and forced geysers of mud and water, from nearby streams, 50 feet into the air. Later a report from shipboard monitoring said, "no radioactivity (was) released to the environment from the underground detonation." Texas Instruments Dallas Services Group was selected to install, operate, and analyze data from ocean bottom seismographs for three weeks to observe aftershock. Amchitka is a 43-mile long volcanic, tectonically unstable island in SW Alaska (Aleutians). According to the Center for Land Use Interpretation, the bomb was 1.2 megatons. Although the test was not a "disaster" it is included as a significant explosion.

The Alcatraz prison, long abandoned by the government, was seized and occupied by a revolving group of Native Americans on November 20, 1969. Though they continued to hold it until 1971 their demands were not really met. They issued the Alcatraz Proclamation asking for a spiritual center and Native American museum at the San Francisco site that had burned down. Citing an 1868 Treaty of Fort Laramie, the occupiers called Indians of All Tribes, claimed a right to Alcatraz, as Native Americans were to receive back all "out of use" federal lands. The government listed Alcatraz as surplus property". They also wanted a center for Native American Studies. The one request that was honored was to put an end to tribal terminations, which closed reservations and moved the occupants to less desirable areas. Another positive effect was the response of the public who often delivered supplies by boat. For most of the time there was no running water, phone, or electricity on Alcatraz. Even celebrities and rock band members helped the cause. One of the organizers and a professor at Berkeley, Dr. La Nada Boyer, said," the occupation was the seed of an effort to rebuild Indian cultures and political alliances among tribes".

THE BLACK PANTHERS

On January 17, 1969 two members of the Black Panther Party, Alprentice "Bunchy" Carter, and John Huggins were murdered on the UCLA campus. A witness account (referenced below) reports that a 21-year-old black male, Claude "Chuchessa" Hubert shot Huggins and then Carter was killed. A former Black Panther describes the use of Special Weapons Tactics teams in subsequent raids on Black Party headquarters. It may have been the first time SWAT teams were used. The FBI, throughout the year as an attempt to weaken the black power movement, increasingly targeted members of the Black Panthers. On December 4, 1969, police in Chicago (not FBI) fired through the door of the apartment of Black Panthers, Fred Hampton, 21, and Mark Clark, 22, killing them and injuring several others. References are below also. I do not include any references to former Attorney General (2009–2015), Eric Holder, who was a member of the Student Afro-American Society at Columbia University in his freshman year (1969–70). Sources disagree as to the degree of involvement he had in persuading the administration to rename an empty NROTC building the "Malcolm X Lounge".

> Pool, Bob, Times staff writer, "Witness to 1969 UCLA shooting speaks at rally" articles.latimes.com Jan 18, 2008.
>
> Roman, Gabriel San, Truthout, "1969:The Year the Black Panther Party was to be Annihilated", Tues, January 28, 2014, 10:22, truthout.org
>
> It's About Time, "Black Panther Party Pieces of History: 1966–69".
>
> History.com-police-kill-two-members-of-the-black-panther-party, Dec.4, 1969
>
> African American Registry, Mon 12-08-1969 through Associated Press.
>
> Blackpast.org/Eric Holder

CHAPTER TWENTY

TAX REFORM—BORING ALERT

The IRS didn't make significant changes to personal income tax in 1969, but foundations (charitable organizations had new sets of rules with the Tax Reform Act of 1969.

It included the following:

*Defining a foundation as a charitable organization that did not engage in inherently public activities, test for public safety or receive substantial report from a wide array of public sources

*The two types of private foundations were operating and non-operating

- Established excise taxes on investment income

*Non-operating foundations were required to distribute 5% of the value of its endowment each year

- Increased existing charitable deduction limits for individual donors.

Leave it to the IRS to define something by what it's not, right?

A foundation can be neither a "for profit" business ownership nor for the private benefit of any individual.

Some examples of non-operating foundations are The Rockefeller Foundation and The Bill and Melinda Gates Foundation.

Operating foundations would be like American Cancer Society Inc. and The World Wildlife Fund.

In 1969, the Keybank Foundation, founded as Key Foundation provided grants, sponsorships, matching gifts, community leadership gifts and volunteer awards through their "Neighbors Make the Difference Day" campaign. Also the Mordag Foundation was established in 1969 with money from Agnes E. Ober in Minnesota.

The only effect on the average person was higher allowance for contributions to these charitable organizations. The effect on tax attorneys and accountants was much greater, of course.

An unfortunate effect of the reform was that painters, sculptors and other artists who donated their works to museums were only allowed to claim the cost of materials used in their work and not a fair market value. Contributions to museums and galleries went down as much as 90% as a result.

CHAPTER TWENTY-ONE

GUNS

Briefly, the 1968 Gun Control Law prohibited convicted felons, drug users, and the mentally ill from buying guns. It also raised the legal age to 21 and expanded licensing requirements for gun dealers. In 1969 an estimated 90 million Americans owned firearms with half of households owning at least one weapon. Nixon Administration representatives saw no need for tighter gun laws. They argued there was no proof of need.

The Gun Control Act didn't apply to long guns such as rifles and shotguns. A look at the titles of some of the articles in the popular magazine, American Rifleman reveals the following:

May, 1969–"A Range that Makes Safety a Habit"

July, 1969–"Let's See Who Backs this Handgun Control" and "Punish Criminals, Not Guns"

September, 1969–"Target Range on the Moon?" "Bullet could Go 279 miles"

October, 1969–"NRA Starts New Hunting Guide Service"

November, 1969–"Jefferson's Beloved Guns" "How they were Restored"

December, 1969–"Crime Higher in Gun Control Cities"

Around July 28, the Violence Commission proposed a licensing system for handguns where a buyer had to prove need and also recommended government confiscation of all unlicensed guns with the government paying for seized guns. Senator Thomas J. Dodd (D-CT) said of that, "I don't think America is ready to go that far." In spite of some control, of 196 police officers killed in 1969, 103 were due to gunfire. The "Officer Down Memorial Page" lists each officer and whether shot accidentally or by another shooter. Finally, OJJDP reports that "Since 1969, homicides involving firearms have been the leading cause of death for African-American males ages 15–19".

CHAPTER TWENTY-TWO

FUTURE BILLIONAIRES

STEVE JOBS

To put a timeline perspective to things, think about the fact that Steve Jobs was a freshman at Homestead High School in Cupertino, California in 1969. There were no personal computers and certainly smart phones hadn't made an appearance since cell phones hadn't been invented yet. But an important friendship came about that year which ultimately helped the development of both PC's and Apple phones. Steve Jobs, 13, started hanging out with Steve Wozniak (frequently just called Woz), a 19 year old engineering student. The two of them shared a love of electronics, Bob Dylan, and pulling pranks. Later Jobs attended Reed College for one semester but eventually quit to join a hippie commune, the All-One Farm, which cultivated of all things, apples. For some time Steve Jobs only ate apples, believing only eating fruit was the healthiest choice. He ended up with a job at Atari that partially helped fund a trip to India ("for enlightenment") for him but he returned disillusioned and more interested in Wozniak's activities with the Home brew Computer Club. Much later of course came success and high income with Apple, Inc. for the two friends who met in 1969.

SAM WALTON

Although there were no Walmarts in Cupertino California for Jobs and Wozniak to buy electronic parts from, there were 24 stores in Arkansas, one in Sikeston, Missouri and another in Claremore, Oklahoma that were part of the October 1969 incorporation of Walmart Stores Inc. Starting with one Ben Franklin franchise store, Sam Walton and his brother J.L. (Bud) Walton, acquired 13 more before opening their own store, Walmart Discount City in Rogers, Arkansas in 1962. After that they typically opened stores in towns with populations of 5,000 to 25,000 keeping advertising costs low with less than 12 promotions per year. The Ben Franklin franchise wouldn't let Sam Walton slash prices as low as he wanted but he made sure Walmarts were known for super low prices. Today, Walmart is the largest private employer in the world with 2.2 million employees (associates) and is still a family owned business. After Sam's death, Christy Walton became the richest woman in the world and Alice Walton is among the top 100 female billionaires also.

OPRAH WINFREY

The only black billionaire in the U.S., Oprah Winfrey was born on January 29, 1952 in poverty. Her childhood was a struggle and she reports being raped at age nine and abused by family. Two years before 1969, she ran away and became pregnant a year later but the child died in infancy. Although dates aren't exact she was at Lincoln High School when she got transferred to the Nicolet High School, a prestigious school where students ridiculed her poverty. She lived with the man she calls father, Vernon, and joined the speech team. She placed 2nd in the nation in dramatic interpretation, won an orating contest, and obtained a full scholarship to Tennessee State

University. At age 17, in 1971, she won Miss Black Tennessee and attracted the attention of a local radio station, WVOL, who gave her a part-time job. Today she is known for philanthropy, spiritual leadership, acting, the Angel Network, and something called "the Oprah effect". It is based on the fact that her beliefs and endorsements have the power to influence everything from book sales and beef markets to political voting. Her net worth is $3.1 billion according to Forbes (#211 on Forbes 400).

DONALD TRUMP

Unlike Oprah, Donald Trump inherited wealth. The Chairman and President of The Trump Organization, Trump Plaza Associates, and Trump Atlantic City Association, worked for his father's firm, Elizabeth Trump and Son, in 1968 after graduation from U. of Penn's Wharton School with a B.S. in economics. In 1971 he took control of the company and changed the name to The Trump Organization. Some of his opponents have tried to label him as a draft dodger because he got deferments after 1969 but he has said he had a very high draft lottery number. It is true that in the December 1969 draft his number was 356. His net worth according to Forbes is $4.5 billion although he says it is higher. He is #121 on Forbes 400 but only #30 on top 100 celebrities while Oprah is #4.

WARREN BUFFETT

The most significant thing in 1969 concerning this powerful partner in Berkshire Hathaway and Diversified Retailing Company, Inc. was his May 1969 letter to his partners outlining his intention to retire and liquidate the partnership. He said, "opportunities for investment had virtually disappeared and he wanted to give all limited partners formal notice". He "found the game no longer worth playing". On year later, however, he was chairman of the board of Berkshire Hathaway. Warren Buffett is #2 on the Forbes 400 and worth $64.6 billion at age 85.

BILL GATES

Did you guess that he was #1 in Forbes's ranking? Growing up in Seattle, he was raised in a warm, close family environment, liking to play Risk and Monopoly with them. His mother, Mary, was civic minded and served on the boards of several charities. In 1969 he attended the Lakeside school where he met Paul Allen, two years older than him but who shared an interest in programs. Gates and Allen were banned from Computer Center Corporation for exploiting bugs to obtain free computer time, but later CCC let them find bugs for them in exchange for time to study source codes and use the computer. That continued until 1970 when CCC went out of business. Although he later dropped out of Harvard, Gates scored 1590 out of 1600 on the SAT in high school. Bill Gates has a net worth of $79.4 billion (Forbes 2015) and is the richest person in the United States.

CHAPTER TWENTY-THREE

SOME THINGS DON'T CHANGE MUCH

Young people may shake their heads and comment how good it is that so much has changed for the better since 1969. It has. But at least one thing remains almost constant today–the weather.

JULY 20, 1969

Reports of the Apollo 11 launch say that it took place "in flawless weather" not unlike many July days now. But over in Houston (as in "Houston we have a problem") the Farmer's Almanac reported that day as foggy, with light drizzle and thunder. The temperature at a high of 84° was similar to the 71° at La Guardia Airport in New York City. The fog, rain, and drizzle reached New York on July 21.

A MAY DAY

Some research at the weather-history.findthebest.com site shows the weather at hundreds of cities in the U.S. on May 31, 1969. As you'd expect most places from Maine to California had temperatures in the 70s and little or no rain. Extremes of 28° in Barrow Alaska and 106° in Chandler, Arizona are not surprising as those lows and highs are common today. In New York, the hottest day of the year was May 29, when it was 96°, but August was the hottest month. But enough about New York weather–there's a whole site at weatherspark.com devoted to 1969 weather there. While monsoons were hampering troop movement in Vietnam, much of the U.S. woke up to beautiful mornings and days in May. In late summer, though, a category 5 storm caused deaths, damage and devastation.

CAMILLE

Hurricane Camille reached landfall in Waveland, Mississippi with at least 175 mile per hour winds on August 17, 1969. The storm killed 259 people, destroyed 5662 homes and did major damage to another 13,915 structures, including the Richelieu apartments in Pass Christian. Hollywood, as it is known to do, made a movie about a supposed hurricane party on the roof but a survivor says that it is false and the only truth is that some residents were killed by the hurricane.

For four or five days, Camille dominated the atmosphere from the Gulf Coast inland through the Appalachian Mountains of Virginia and east to Norfolk. Extensive flooding and damage occurred while Camille crossed the mountains before interacting with Hurricane Debbie and a cold front that changed it into an extra tropical cyclone with cooler air. Many residents of Mississippi later complained that they weren't given strong enough warning about the storm which inspired the implementation of the Saffir-Simpson Hurricane Scale in 1969 to make warnings clearer.

SNOW

How often is the National Weather Service wrong? Though that's debatable, on February 9, 1969, the NWS forecast a change to rain that afternoon just before 15 inches of snow fell in the East, most of it in New York City. 42 people were killed and the city shut down. Blocked and snow-drifted roadways had residents barricaded in their homes. Mayor John Lindsay was severely criticized for ineffective snow removal measures and defective equipment and 288 people reported injuries connected with the storm. For three days there were no buses, cabs, trash collection or deliveries.

The East was hit again by another nor'easter around December 25. The storm was a Category 3 or 4 on the Northeast Snowfall Impact Scale and caused blocked roadways and 20 deaths from Washington, D.C. to New England.

However, the weather, at both those times in California, was sunny and clear.

CHAPTER TWENTY-FOUR

YOU DON'T GET MORE "BACK TO THE LAND" THAN FARMS

What the United States has more of, other than people, than anything else would be land. The USDA 1969 census lists total acres at 2,263,680,000 of which 53% is in farms (1,063,346,000 acres) with an average size farm of 7,591.7 acres, concentrated most in the West and South, and then in the North Central regions of the country. Cropland is largest in the Corn Belt, naturally. Besides land used to grow crops, there are dairy farms, livestock producers and poultry farms which include pasture and grazing land which comprise 39.6% of the total U.S. available land. Although an analysis of farm economics is not a focus here, a University of Minnesota Report on 147 dairy farms puts the average cost per cow for feeding, housing and other expenses at $703 in 1969. I think my parents paid about that for my first college term that year–hmm).

In addition to dairy farms, there were 1.7 million cattle-producing farms but the number was down from previous years and continued to decline, while Frank Perdue took to the radio with ads for chicken (68–69). The Big Four packinghouses for meat were Swift, Armour, Cudahy, and Wilson, but many of the new fast food chains bought chicken. Some companies entered into agreements with farmers to produce a certain amount of tomatoes, chickens, or wheat, providing feed and supplies, taking on a big part of the risk but making most of the farming decisions called "contract farming", while others took their chances with the open market. In addition to 3,537 "7-eleven" stores selling food, supermarkets had 70% of the retail food business and the farms should have been quite lucrative. One problem however, was the drain on labor from the war. Over two million men left rural areas and farms for Vietnam. The number of man-hours recorded in 1969 was 6.9 billion for livestock production, 104 billion for crops, and 4 billion for maintenance. Farmers moved on and got support from many groups such as the Iowa Beef Packers, Nebraska Pork Producers Association, and The National Soybean Association.

Like car and car engine enthusiasts, farmers might be a little obsessed with tractors. Considering though that a horse team would take more than 50 hours to plow a forty-acre field and a tractor (pulling a 26-ft disc harrow unit) could do it in about an hour, it is understandable. Forget Chrysler, Dodge, and Ford Mustang, ask a farmer about the 1969 Allis Chalmers Model Twenty Two Land Handler that had beefed up transmission and a heavier rear end to handle pulls and the J.I. Case 1969 tractor Model 2670 that could produce 219 horsepower. Big names in tractors were John Deere, who developed "Roll-Gard" after 100's of farmers died in rollover accidents on high centered machines, International Harvester, Ford, and Minneapolis-Moline.

Of course, like cars, tractors were sometimes used for sport. The tractor pull was not new in 1969 but it was introduced to the world at The National Farm Equipment Show and originator Billy Joe Miles created the WBHM and the National Tractor Pullers Association was established. There were sixty-six tractors in three classes from 5000 to 15000 pounds to pull a sled with increasing friction. Unlike NASCAR, the goal was not speed but distance pulled.

"FARMS?"

The following are not really farms but more communal living places.
Many ancient civilizations worshiped the Sun (Egyptians), Moon (Incas) or the Earth and Sky (Native Americans) so it was somewhat understandable that many young people would be inspired by nature. Thinking of starting Utopia, some hippies settled in communes across the country. In the New Buffalo commune in New Mexico, Indian Sikh Yogi Bhajan taught Yoga as part of a spiritual awakening. Some commune members rejected drugs and began a ritual of meditation and chanting. Spontaneity, playfulness, and openness were cherished.

A teacher, who lost his job for protesting the war, started a commune in Georgeville, Minnesota.

An archeological dig unearthed the remnants of a hippie commune (Olompali), which indicated a group of 50–70 people ages 17–50 had lived in a 24-room mansion and several nearby structures in 1967–1969 before it was destroyed by fire. They found remnants of albums: Super Session by Mike Bloomfield, Al Kooper, and Stephen Stills, West Side Story, Beethoven Symphony # 3 and Ella Fitzgerald Sings the Gershwin Songbook.

The Hog Farm, still in existence today in California with headquarters in Berkeley is the longest running hippie commune. Wavy Gravy, the clown and peace activist who provided security and food at Woodstock, founded it. Whether actual farming goes on there is not documented, but they do run Camp Winnarainbow for kids there and teach juggling, unicycling, and tightrope walking among other things.

In 1969 there were 640,000 farms with actual hog sales.

CHAPTER TWENTY-FIVE

FLOWER CHILDREN, BODY ART, AND PATCHOULI

Sometimes flower child was used interchangeably for hippie and there was little distinction between the two. Flower children had simple idealistic values. They grew in numbers in the 1967 Summer of Love and were immortalized in Scott McKenzie's ballad telling young people to "be sure and wear some flowers in your hair" (if you're going to San Francisco). Their life styles included gender equality, communal living and free love while striving for gentleness. This is not to say that flower children or hippies didn't use drugs. Drug use was in full bloom in 1969. A Jungian interpretation by Robert Anton Wilson in his book <u>Prometheus Rising</u> is that these young people displayed "a mood of friendly weakness". The term "flower power" may have come from Allen Ginsburg as a power of passive resistance. A suggested comparison between the flower-bestowing Eloi (vs. Morlock) in H.G. Wells' <u>Time Machine</u> is not supported by documentation. (In the book and movie, the creepy Morlock race worked underground to provide an idyllic, hedonistic world for the Eloi above. It soon becomes clear that the Eloi (adults) were like defenseless children and that the Morlock were killing and consuming them one by one). Photos from 1967 and 1968 show a few hippies placing flowers in gun barrels, but activism, not passivity was on the rise in 1969.

BODY ART

You've seen sports fans paint their faces or body for a big game, I'm sure. It was only occasionally, though, that you saw body art in 1969. However, it was more frequent at music concerts and art festivals. Using liquid latex or water-based paints flowers, peace symbols, designs, or words were painted on partially clothed young people often to get attention for a particular political or social cause. This type of body art should not be confused with the technique of having a nude model roll in paint and then lie on a canvas, which was tried in Europe, mostly. Actress Judy Carne often had words and pictures painted on her swimsuit-clad body on the TV show "Laugh-In". The paint used was a thick and durable watercolor that had to hold up under studio lights. The camera zoomed in on particular words when she stopped dancing. Pinterest has many photos of body painting if you want to see examples. Temporary tattoos, especially of the hands, were done with henna, which lasted about two weeks. Though body painting, piercing, and tattoos were around many centuries ago, they had renewed popularity in 1969.

PATCHOULI

Although this is made from flowers grown in Indonesia, India, Thailand and Vietnam, the perfume does not come out smelling like a rose. When you look up "patchouli" in the Urban Dictionary the definition is "hippie perfume". The incense made with it and the perfumes were popular with hippies in 1969. The woody, musty smell was supposed to cover up the smell of marijuana smoke, but it was so strong it was sometimes a "tell". A 59 year old in 2007 recalled that he wore patchouli because it wasn't his father's scent. Trying to distance themselves many hippies rejected everything about their parents' lives, including their chosen smell. Many people liked to burn patchouli incense, but the truth is not everyone liked the smell. In 1985, patchouli oil in the plastic was used to make Stinkor in The Mattel Masters of The Universe toy series.

CHAPTER TWENTY-SIX

GUITARS AND SITARS

One of the easiest instruments to play, the guitar can be carried on the back and propped up almost anywhere when not being played. It's no wonder it was popular in 1969 and continues to be today. However, not all places welcomed guitar music. Many Christian churches didn't want to include them fearing an onslaught of rock music and all the other types of music of the day such as soul, jazz, and pop music. Citing the solemnity of the church services, one Ministry writer (Seventh Day Adventist) wrote that the guitar music would detract from the service and do nothing to contribute to the worship environment. Still non-amplified guitars found their way into some churches, often by way of weddings where the bride and groom requested it. Peter Paul and Mary's "There is Love" (wherever two or more of us are gathered in His name) was often sung with guitar accompaniment. Outside of church, though, it was common to have a guitar playing, "If I Had A Hammer", "Blowin' in The Wind" or "Where Have All the Flowers Gone?" at festivals, peace rallies, and campfires. Churches, however, were looking for contemporary songs "with a message" that was God-centered. Larry Norman was the first musician to combine rock rhythms with the Christian message in 1969.

1969 was the first year that the National Endowment for the Arts gave any support at all to jazz and folk music. The electric guitar was not usually allowed in churches, but one Chicago Lutheran Church held a guitar laboratory in 1969 for neighborhood young people 11 to 15. A $27,000 Title I grant funded the program where amplifiers were turned off during practice. The program instructor commented, "everyone wants to play guitar since the Beatles became popular".

The sitar was introduced to many young people when Ravi Shankar played at Woodstock. The instrument was previously popular with those who were fascinated by India. Mostly hippies, some fans of sitar music also embraced the food and philosophies of the Eastern culture, but Ravi Shankar was quoted later as saying that the 60's "got India all wrong". In a Rolling Stone interview, Shankar said, "I want clear-headed, physically and mentally clean people when they listen". He did not like it when young people got stoned or high on LSD and then listened to his music hoping for visions or enhanced highs. His popularity only diminished slightly even though he distanced himself from the hippie movement. One of his students in 1965 was George Harrison, who played sitar on the Beatle's song "Norwegian Wood" and "Within You Without You" on the Sgt. Pepper Lonely Hearts album. Other artists used the sitar in "Green Tambourine", "Didn't I Blow Your Mind This Time" ('69 Delfonics) and "Carpet Man" (5th Dimension). A song by Elvis Presley included sitar music, also.

Limiting the scope of this book to 1969, many trends, especially in music, are too numerous to cover. The reference section in the back of the book includes sites that provide more information for interested readers. "Hippies from A TO Z" by Skip Stone on hipplanet.com is very thorough with events, people, names, best locations, and a glossary of slang. Music of 1969, pop, psychedelic, rock, and classical, can be found on dozens of sites as well.

CHAPTER TWENTY-SEVEN

EDUCATION AND 'SAVING' TVPBS

Schools in 1969 faced much more serious issues than enforcing common dress codes of dresses and skirts for girls and no jeans or T-shirts for boys. As baby boomers matured, class size began to increase adding to teacher problems. In May, the Chicago Teacher's Union made the Tribune headline with it's first strike after The Board of Education proposed cutting 7000 positions, increasing class size and teaching load and eliminating some educational services. Settling after a few days the union secured the guaranteed employment of 900 teacher aids in high schools and another 900 elementary school aides. Elementary teachers earned two daily preparation periods and class size maximums were set (30/primary, 33/intermediate, and 35/upper grades). However problems still existed in places other than Chicago.

While protest in 1969 usually brings to mind unrest at colleges and universities, the beginnings of protest and even rage by parents of school age children grew over the issue of busing to integrate schools. A long history of segregation didn't help promote change in the South, obviously. For example the Charlotte-Mecklenburg School District (NC) West Charlotte School was all black until 1969. Described as the "least endowed school" of the district, the school used second hand and battered supplies while white schools had new, functioning ones. A proposal to begin the ordered desegregating in the 1969–70 school year entailed shutting down the all black school and busing students to white areas, but the district was forced to revise the plan. The cost of transportation rose from $542,000 to $2,000,000 annually and some students rode 35–75 miles to school. White parents formed the Concerned Parents Association and obtained 20,000 signatures against busing. On the other side of the country in Seattle, Washington, African American parents also responded in their area by forming the Central Area School Council to promote community control of public schools and improve them rather than ship students across the city. Eventually every major city across the country from Boston to Chicago to Pasadena encountered problems with school integration, looking for alternatives to forced busing. However, the Chicago Tribune reported that a student who missed the chartered bus one morning actually walked five miles to get to school. That has got to rival the "walked one mile uphill to school–both ways– when I was young" story.

PBS

Though Sesame Street's popularity soared all over the world, Mr. Rogers Neighborhood was often ridiculed especially when Eddie Murphy spoofed him and his show in a recurring Saturday Night Live skit. He was unique and soft-spoken but did his best to counteract violent cartoons and promote healthy attitudes in children. He not only taught them to hang up their sweater instead of tossing it on a chair, but gave children an understanding of their feelings and introduced them to how factories made ordinary things and how construction worked.

Following six years in child development, dealing with children's inner drama, Fred Rogers went before the Senate Subcommittee on Communications to obtain funds for the Corporation for Public Broadcasting on May 1, 1969. He didn't read the prepared ten-minute written philosophical statement saying that just as children learn trust, Rogers trusted that the chairman and his committee would read it. Instead he recited the words to one of his songs ("What Do You Do with the Mad that You Feel"). His gentle, soothing voice had already caused Chairman John Pastore to say he had goose bumps, and when Mr. Rogers finished, Mr. Pastore responded, "Looks like you just earned twenty million dollars". The actual appropriation that year was only five million, but Rogers is credited with the twenty-two million that came in 1971.

CHAPTER TWENTY-EIGHT

RELIGION IN 1969

Oh boy, having learned a long time ago to avoid discussing politics and religion if you don't want an argument, I'm jumping in anyway.

A report for the Journal of Scientific Study of Religion says 42% of the white population of America reported having gone to church in the last seven days in 1969. They base it on a Gallup poll that doesn't specify sample size or who was sampled. Mentioning anti-establishment views in 1969, the Gallup poll estimates church attendance was down 9 to 11 points from 1955 and 5 points below the 1955 figure for Protestants.

On February 14, 1969 as a result of Vatican II, 93 saints were dropped from the General Roman Calendar. Included were St. Valentine, St. George, St. Nicholas, and the very popular St. Christopher, patron saint of travelers and motorists. Although some people were upset because they misunderstood and thought these saints were no longer saints (decanonized). However most of those saints had received the title of saint in a time before the modern papal process of canonization existed. Since they were not canonized, no de-canonization could take place. The reasons for dropping them had more to do with doubts of their existence and the crowded Roman calendar. They are still saints but celebration of their feast days was left to local calendars. Catholics were not discouraged from invoking them in prayers.

ALTERNATIVES

Billy Graham, Kathryn Kuhlman and Pat Robertson were on television for some to "go to church" in their own living room, but not many young people considered that an option. Billy Graham, as White House Chaplain under Nixon, was considered too pro-war for hippies. In an April 15, 1969 letter to the president he suggested bombing dikes across North Vietnam if the Paris Peace Talks failed to end the war. Later it was estimated that would have killed one million North Vietnamese. To his credit, though, he helped end segregation by telling a KKK member that, "there is no biblical basis for segregation". He was not in favor of feminism considering it "an echo of the overall philosophy of permissiveness". However, he preached that Christianity was something you had to grow into, even after converting, and some found wisdom in that. Billy Graham has his own star on the Hollywood Walk of Fame, but I suspect he values a place in heaven much more. All in all, though, Billy Graham was a revered evangelist for his beliefs and crusades for Christianity.

Some young people chose Buddhism and eastern philosophies for alternative spirituality. Zen Buddhism came to the U.S. in 1969 and the first Tibetan Buddhist center was established at Berkeley, but very few hippies actually practiced the religion strictly. More popular was the teaching of Maharishi Mahesh Yogi who practiced Transcendental Meditation. Both the Beatles and The Beach Boys traveled with him and followed his methods for a while. The guru said in an interview that TM "was necessary to dissolve stress". Daily yoga is a requirement for "the existence of a fourth state of consciousness with a basis in physiology". Maharishi Yogi was a vegetarian and a monk who didn't drink, smoke, or do drugs. Much of the mysticism and alternative spirituality was most popular in California. Meanwhile, back in Maine, the Midwest, and South, members of traditional churches worshiped and did charitable and missionary work as usual. However, Catholics, Methodists, Baptists, Episcopalians, Presbyterians, and many others did not advertise their good works or record them publicly in 1969 to be cited. The decline in their church attendance that year was only slight.

Like the chicken or the egg question, it's hard to know whether young adults blamed organized religion for strictness, stands against birth control and being for the war as why they left the church or if the church blamed drug use, hippies, Woodstock, and protests for pulling young people away from church. Although I don't know the answer and it isn't germane to this book's moderate approach, here's a quote, from a poster on Nature's Herb Forum (www.herbs.mxf.yuku.com) The man, 59, when he posted (anonymous with an Hendrix avatar) on November 9, 2007 went off topic from "why patchouli was associated with hippies?" to give a possible answer to the question above. He said, "The straight people and the hippies were both closed minded, just closed minded in different directions." He goes on to call the "us and them" attitude back then silly and ends with "The good values from both sides are a strong part of today".

CHAPTER TWENTY-NINE

INVENTORS AND SCIENTISTS

In 2016, we take our flat screen TV, laptop, cell phone battery storage, and Prius hybrid cars in stride, but these things came about slowly and in great part due to the work of a man featured in Life Magazine on October 17, 1969. Stanford R. Ovshinsky was an innovator and even without a college degree might have been "the Edison of the age" as was the proposed title by the British newspaper, "The Economist". Born in Akron Ohio, he went public in 1968, announcing he had discovered "the Ovshinsky effect" (naming it after himself of course) which involved the transformation of a nonconductive glassy thin film to a semiconductor with the application of a certain minimum voltage. In the past he had done pioneering work in examples of nanostructures and energy storage. His life as a scientist blossomed however in 1969 and onward as ovonic switches became a better alternative than transistors, which were made of perfect crystals and were difficult to produce. Ten renowned scientists joined Ovshinsky and backed up his work, causing his discovery to be featured in the Wall Street Journal, The New York Times, and Life Magazine.

Light panels activated by tiny ovonic switches could make it possible to produce a flat wall TV. The new brand of physics called "ovionics" from the self-taught engineer was not all Ovshinsky worked on both in 1969 and later years. He obtained over 200 U.S. patents and wrote over 300 publications on the generation, collection, and storage of energy (including solar energy), high capacity batteries and electric vehicles.

Dr. George Caruthers, an African American physicist was awarded a patent on November 11,1969 for an Image Converter. It was used for detecting electromagnetic radiation, especially in short wave length. His doctorate from the University of Illinois was in aeronautical and astronomical engineering and he provided valuable input to later Apollo missions.

In medical science, two "firsts" occurred in 1969 that were beneficial to future advancements despite the fact that they weren't complete successes. The patient who received the first artificial heart transplant by Dr. Denton Cooley in Houston only lived with it for sixty-four hours before a human heart transplant became necessary. He survived only two days after that. The first human eye transplant on April 22, 1969 was considered a success but it didn't restore the patients eyesight.

The 1969 Nobel Prize in Physiology or Medicine went to three men: Max Delbruck, Alfred D. Hershey, and Salvador Luria. Their study of bacteriophages provided a deeper insight into the nature of viruses and virus diseases. Though Delbruck and Luria came to the U.S. from Berlin and Italy respectively, Hershey, an American microbiological chemist, had used bacteriophages for years as an antigen in immunological reaction studies.

A total of 1,835,000 scientists, engineers, and technicians worked in the United States in 1969, excluding psychologists and social scientists and including 210,303 who worked in the federal government. Engineers numbered 849,000; technicians 772,500; and chemists 90,500, with mathematicians and physicists representing about 39,000 people each. It seems there were a lot of "Sheldon Coopers" and a few "Amy Farrah Fowlers" that year. From the 1972 census, 15,993 science doctorates were conferred in 1969 and 13.1 % went to females. (The 1971 census lists 15,982 science doctorates in 1969). Doctorates in psychology and social sciences were 1728 and 1951, respectively.

Previous chapters have included the magnetic strip and ATM inventions, but there are several inventions and patents that also came about in 1969. Intel Corporation introduced the world's first metal oxide semi-conductor, the 1101, and also the 3101 Schottky bipolar 64-bit static random access memory chip. The 3101 was twice as fast as earlier chips. Maria Van Brittan Brown received US patent 3,482,037 for a home security system using television on December 2, 1969. Devices of this type are still used in apartment and office buildings to "see who is at the door". David N. Crosthwait, the electrical and mechanical engineer who created the heating system for Radio City Music Hall, retired in 1969 but held many patents including ones for vacuum pumps and thermostat components. He taught steam heating and control systems at Purdue University, later receiving an honorary doctorate. In all 194,357 US patents were applied for in 1969 and 71,229 others were issued. (For clarity, it should be noted that the figures as given have no relationship to one another as any or all patents issued could have been applied for in previous years).

Prior to 1969, the United States Navy, which guarded the coast of Antarctica at point of entry McMurdo Station, refused to transport women to the continent. The National Science Foundation wouldn't consider research proposals from women regarding Antarctica either. But in 1969, the Navy lifted the ban and the NSF began accepting research applications for Antarctica from women. This prompted Ohio State University's Department of Polar Studies to assemble an Antarctica research team headed by geochemist, Dr. Lois Jones. Also included were Eileen McSaveney, a glacial geology expert, Kay Lindsay, an entomologist, Terry Tickhill Terrell, a 19-year-old science student, Pam Young, biologist, and Jean Pearson, a science writer for the Detroit News. The women were all "first women" to the South Pole because on November 12, 1969 they jumped off the back of their cargo plane onto the Pole at the same time to make it so. Further research reveals, though, that Christine Muller-Schwarze, a Utah State University PhD in Psychology studied penguins at Cape Crozier, Antarctica in October 1969 with her scientist husband. Although two sources refer to her as "the first woman scientist to work in the U.S. Antarctic Research Program" the following from The Antarctic Journal of The United States Research Program does not specifically mention it.

"An historic event was the arrival of the first women scientists to work on the continent as part of the U.S. Antarctica Research Program. Women of many nations preceded them… most others had been there in such capacities as wives of explorers, ships crew, reporters and tourists… they (these women scientists) were the first women ever to visit the South Pole Station"

Tidbits–(Because an hour of research and pages of notes often boil down to a sentence or two.)

The first year Aids was possibly observed in the United States was 1969, although the boy who died from it was not diagnosed as such until tissue samples were tested in later years.

In 1969, Gary Starkweather had the idea to use a laser beam to draw an image onto a copier drum. His work in Xerox's product development department was actualized in 1971.

Majestic Prince won the Kentucky Derby in 1969.

Prize winning recipes in that year included green bean salad, spicy sausage sauerbraten sandwich, and dump cake.

Popular department stores (which later became part of Macy's) were: Lazarus, Filene's, Bullock's, Jordan Marsh, Kaufmann's, Marshall Field's, Rich's, and Stern's.

The fourth and current building of the U.S. Mint opened in Philadelphia in 1969. As of January 2009 it was the world's largest mint.

On June 28.1969, patrons of The Stonewall inn in New York City, tired of harassment by police for liquor license, dress, and dance violations took a stand and a riot ensued. That all of the customers were members of the gay community and that the establishment was Mafia owned is not clearly confirmed or denied, but the incident is recognized as the start of the Gay Liberation Front and the gay rights movement.

By the end of the 60's (1969) American youths had spent an estimated $20 million on posters in Op Art. Peter Max was a popular designer of posters, tableware, clothes, and even city buses. He said he learned "love, harmony, unity, and symmetry under Yoga".

Allowing the counter culture to laugh a little at their actions, a source says that Gary Trudeau won syndication for "Doonesbury" in 1969. Others say that an agent for United Press did offer syndication but it was for Trudeau's Yale Comic strip, "Bull Tale's", which was later renamed "Doonesbury".

The Supreme Court of Appeals reversed a verdict against the Founding Church of Scientology, Washington, D.C. for property (booklets and E-meters which gave a mild shock) seized by U.S. Marshalls earlier. The Court ruled that the Church had made a substantial showing that it was a religion and the government had not rebutted the claim.

DDT was essentially banned for all household and residential use in 1969 when the USDA denied applications for its use.

Samuel Beckett won the Nobel Prize for Literature that year.

In the population of America, 73.6% over sixteen-year-olds held driver's licenses. (87% of the males and 61.5% of the females. A Motor Fuel inspection law was enacted in 1969 to provide for the inspection and testing of motor fuel products. Gas was thirty-two cents a gallon.

Among 1969 patents was one for a memory control system on April 2, 1969.

John Ostrom published a monograph on the Deinonychas dinosaur he discovered in 1964. He presented his findings at the American Paleontological Convention in Chicago in 1969 and fueled the belief that birds were descended from dinosaurs.

Cybil Shepherd was the Breck Girl (after Cheryl Tiegs 1968). Breck was a sponsor of America's Junior Miss Competition. In the 70's, though, the Breck Girl was seen as a "liability".

In Art, the Andrew Dickson White Museum of Art (predecessor to Cornell's Johnson MOA) presented an Earth Art exhibit of

"Earthworks" in early 1969. Artists used the earth itself as canvas or sculpture material. This had an impact on future artists working on ecology related works.

The Dance Theatre of Harlem, a professional dance company, was founded by Arthur Mitchell and Kerel Shook in 1969 to give children the same opportunities Mitchell had as a teenager.

The mandatory isolation and forced quarantine of the Kalaupapa community in Hawaii was abolished in 1969. Hansen's disease (leprosy) had been eliminated by sulfa drugs decades earlier but many Hawaiians still lived there voluntarily. It is now a National Historic Park.

SUMMARY

Many effects of 1969 came about slowly from seeds planted that year. And, as in nature, some seeds did not produce good growth. The invention of a crude TV Ping-Pong game did not immediately launch a billion dollar video game industry any more than a small number of hippies on communes expanded organic farming and eating preservative-free foods to its current level. No people live on the moon and war has not disappeared. However, the ideas became a starting point in the process of change. As a whole, the year doesn't fit the definition of a pivotal or boom year and didn't always react as a catalyst in the process of growth from past years. Ideally though, 1969 could be called a planting year for future harvest. ARPANET was certainly the catalyst with CompuServe for the Internet explosion today. The figure for 2016 users changes each second on www.internetlivestats.com and was 3,354,149,300 at time of writing. There are 425,000 ATM's in America and 3,000,000 worldwide (2015) that directly came about from the invention by Donald Wetzel (Docutel) using cards with a magnetic strip developed by IBM, both in 1969.

The trivial influences from body art and piercing set the stage for today's trend in tattoos and piercings while tie-dyed clothes and psychedelic art are seen in patterned leggings and clothing, advertisements, and adult coloring books. The counterculture, which opposed the war and fought for women's rights and civil rights, produced positive growth toward a society, which recognizes equal rights and contributes to lessons learned from the war in Vietnam. We have women CEO's and a female admiral, an Afro-American President and reduced black unemployment. Some activists changed as well. Replacing extreme behavior with trying to work within the system and searching for peace within brought Yoga for relaxation and health, Jazzercise, and healthy eating trends. (Of course, doctors and dieticians played a large part too).

National Policy was changed in 1969 with The Environmental Policy Act of 1969 following the Santa Barbara Oil spill. The International Association Against Painful Experiments on Animals exposed drug experiments on animals. The IAAPEA was founded in 1969. The Tax Reform Act on December 30, 1969 gave greater allowances for charitable contributions and revised the tax on foundations. Coal miners were given assurance of black lung benefits with the Federal Coal Mine and Safety Act of 1969. Mine owners were also required to undergo two inspections per year (four for underground mines) and pay monetary penalties for violations.

Even with all the seeds of change in 1969, without a growth medium, the process would stop. Without going into the sociology or psychology, it might be said that many individuals, taking small steps toward understanding, forgiving, acceptance, fair solutions and maintaining values provided the elements for growth, and others seeking alternatives to condemnation, rage, bigotry, and waste "pulled the weeds" that threatened survival. We should never forget our war heroes, but each person who enabled the process of change with even the smallest of steps, is part of the "leap for mankind" that Neil Armstrong started on July 17, 1969 on the moon. Maybe you, or your parent, or grandparents are one of them.

NOTES

1

Three years of research, writing, and editing should be enough to cover the facts when they are limited to only one year. However, I found something new about 1969 every time I worked on a subject or different aspect. Extrapolating, this process could go on indefinitely and needed to have an end point.

Rather than apologize, I have included a section "Further Reading" after the References section for any reader who wants to learn more about those and other events or 1969 people. Maybe I glossed over the Manson Cult and The Zodiac Killer murders but Rob Kilpatrick's book is more detailed on that. The Yippie movement and leaders Abby Hoffman and Jerry Rubin are also absent, (and they can write or "steal" their own book). I also leave the motivations and reasons for behaviors that year to the psychologists and sociologists. Maybe some of the things people did in 1969 wouldn't hold up well to public scrutiny, or not be what you want to tell your grandchildren, but most people have moved on and hopefully can find much in this book to pass on.

If you want further credentials, other than the bibliography, I have no long list of published papers or books to give you. It probably doesn't matter that I was valedictorian in a 1969 class of over 1000 high school seniors or that I have a B.S., in Mathematics, was a 7–12 public school teacher for sixteen years, or even that I have five published mysteries (fiction) on Amazon and a non-fiction Word press blog called Multi-musings (yes a shameless plug). Although I interject personal observations on a few occasions in this book,

I stick to the facts for the most part. It is important, though, to know that I checked at least two independent sources for entries and checked again when there was a discrepancy. Exceptions are covers or feature article titles from Sports Illustrated, The Rifleman Magazine, and The Chicago Tribune archives. Wikipedia.org use was on a "read only" basis.

2

I deleted a section on "fun" in 1969 because it seemed subjective with no real research to back it up. Things like all-night bowling, volleyball, swimming, and sports, board games, short card games like "spit", "war" and gin rummy were "popular" with some young people; Adult bridge clubs and bingo, sports and vacations to the beach or campsites with the whole family were common. Racing cars and working on engines were favorites of some as were drinking games, fraternity/sorority mixers, and chugging contests at many colleges and universities. (There was information to be found about some states allowing 18 year olds to drink 3.2 beers (lower alcohol content)). It's true there was no karaoke but many people played guitar or piano, went to concerts, movie marathons, or lectures by guest speakers and–though you may laugh–reading for pleasure was enjoyed by people of all ages. Yes, reading! What about drugs? The use of marijuana and mind-altering drugs by less than 10% of the population was a factor in the 1969 equation but it wasn't really a seed for future growth but more of a "weed" factor. Actually jokes were as entertaining in 1969 as always. From the absurd, "Why don't you ever see elephants hiding in trees–because they are really, really good at it" to the annoying, like Knock-Knock, Who's there? Deja, Deja Who? Knock-Knock, Who's there? Deja...

The above-undocumented commentary on life in 1969 is included in Author notes as anecdotal and is not necessarily representative of the social activities of any individual, group or majority.

3

Pomegranates

In 2016, stores offer pure pomegranate juice full of anti-oxidants and many health benefits to be enjoyed without all of the mess of dealing with the rind and the slight bitterness of the pith. I have bought the packaged seed too but it's not like you can eat the whole cup in one sitting like mini-Oreos. So, you sprinkle some on salads, mix them in with your yogurt or cereal and take pleasure in the fact that you're adding a super food to your diet. You can easily Google ten sites that tell you how to eat a pomegranate (first page).

http://www.thepomegranateyear1969.com is preferred over letters.

THE END

REFERENCES

*References are listed by chapter. Online URL's do not include the (http) prefix but most are clickable for online reading as is. The optional citing of "date accessed" is not used.

Introduction

"ARPANET is the First Internet", Article, www.living.com/history

"News and Events of 1969", www.infoplease.com

Archer, Jules: The Incredible Sixties, The Stormy Years that changed America, Harcourt, Brace, and Jovanovich 1986.

Baer, Ralph, H. Smithsonian Institute/national-museum-of-american history/Biography/Ralph-H-Baer

Lunar and Planetary Science, www://lpi.usra.edu/lunar/missions/apollo/apollo_11/

http://nasa.gov/mission_pages/Apollo11.html

http://thepeoplehistory.com, "The Year 1969"

Rodale, Robert, http://rodalesorganiclife.com "The Back to the Land Movement by Robert Rodale, September 1969. Originally published in Organic and Farming Magazine, January 22, 2015.

Gannin, Frank, "Home from the Moon, July 24, 1969 Richard Nixon Foundation, July 23, 2008

Chapter 1–Space

"Could more Russian rocket engine export ban halt US Space Program?" RT News Question, http://onrt.com/aw7iuz, 8/27/2013

Aboutusa.japan.usembassy.gov/e/jusa-environment-space.html

Adamschwartz.hubpages.com/hub/The-Value-of-space-exploration

Delgado, Laura M. "Russia's Space Program Still Relevant" (also used in UFO chapter)

http://spacepolicyonline.com November 4, 2011

Life Magazine 1/10/69 picture of the moon

Life Magazine 11/17/69 pictures of Nasa engineers working on spacecraft

Nasa.gov/mission_pages/apollo/apollo_11/

Schwartz, John, "Space & Cosmos: The Long Countdown, one way up: US Space Plan relies on Russia", New York Times

http://history.nasa.gov/ap11-35ann/apollo11-log/log.htm

YouTube, Landing on the Moon: July20, 1969.

Chapter 2–Home life, meals, cost of living

"An illustrated History of Soul Food" http://festivefeast.com/eat/an-illustrated-history-of-soul-food

http://1960sflashback.com/1969/economy.asp

http://aaregistry.com

http://americanfood.about.com

http://archiveschicagotribune, March 9, 1969, Sept. 25, 1969

http://foodtimeline.org.food.faq?.html (Better Homes and Gardens Oct 1969 cited

http://foodtimeline.org/foodecades.html

http://mprime.com/ProjectFirebird/

http://radar58.com

http://ranker.com/list/list-of-cars-made-in-1969

http://smoop.com/1960s/culture.html

http://thepeoplehistory.com/1969/html

Weissman, Jordan www.slate.com/blogs/moneybox/2014/12/08 "Collapse_of_middle_class_wealth_the_median_family_is_worth _less_today_than_in-1969

Chapter 3 Sports

Adelson, Alan, staff reporter Wall Street Journal, "On wall Street, Mets' fans outdo V-J Day-Lindberg festivities". October 17, 1969.

http://infoplease.com/year/1969.html#sports

http://lifemagazineconnection.com/LIFE magazines-1960s/LIFE -Magazine-Joe Namath January 24, 1969 issue.

Smith, Sandy, "Namath" Life Magazine article 1/24/69.

Senior Living

Sports Illustrated covers 1/12/69, 1/13/69, Namath: "Namath Weeps" on cover 6/16/69

www.biography.com/people/arthur-ashe-919044

www.notablebiographies.com

www.surfingresearch.com.au

www.encyclopediaofsurfing.com

McWhirter, Norris and Ross, The Guinness Book of Records, Guinness Superlatives Limited, Sixteenth Edition, London, 1969, p. 256, p. 26

Chapter 4 Fashion

http://instyle.com/instyle/package/general/photos/9,20475651-204787516–209217817,000html

http://casreport.org/usa/run/richfield/hs/1969

http://www.theguardian.com/notesandqueries/query/10,5753-26861,00.html

http://www.vintagedancer.com/1920s/mens-tie-history-1920s-to-1970s

http://lifetime.com/fashion.life-looks-at-high-school-fashion-circa-1969

Wright, John, tie-a-tie.net/blog/the-evolution-of-the-necktie

Nastasi, Alison, Flavorline "Television Mad Men Style/What are people wearing in 1969/April 12, 2014 1:02 p.m.

Baardwijk, Marjolcin van and Franses, Philip Hans, Hemlines, Monthly Data 1921–2009

Palm Beach Post, Thursday February 25, 1971/Hemlines

Lawrence Kansas Newspapers, "Hemline battle began" March 12, 1969

http://educationfindlaw.com/SchoolDressCodes

Chapter 5 Vietnam

http://www.atic.mil/doctrine/history/jcsvietnam_69-79.pdf

http://marines.mil/Portals/sq/Publications/U.S.%20Marines%20rg%20vietnam

http://www.faculty.rhodes.edu/wetzel/random/draftlottery.html

http://www.rand.com

http://www.landscaper.net/draft.htm#vietnam%20troop%20levels

Faiers, Chris Nov 2002, eelpie.org/cricket/vietnam.htm

http://www.columbia.edu/(tilda)rse14/vietnam_rev_Feb2010.pdf

"What John McCain went through as a POW" http://abcnews.go.com

Alkinson, Gerald L., http://www.newtotalitarianism.com, "John McCain as a Prisoner of War"

http://www.history.com

Arnett, Peter (Pulitzer prize winner, Associated Press), Kerrey, Senator "Bob", (Vietnam veteran, Governor of Nebraska), Miller, Edward G. (Dartmouth college expert), Palmer. Laura (Reporter in Vietnam and Rolling Stone article credit), and Vallely, Thomas J. (Former director of Harvard Vietnam Program and a Vietnam Marine) "Vietnam: New Lessons from an Old War: Fifty years hence", University of Pittsburgh Honors College Symposium, University Club, Oakland PA. March 4, 2014.

Life Magazine, June 27, 1969. "The Faces of the American Dead in Vietnam"

Patti, Archimedes, <u>Why Vietnam? Prelude to America's Albatross.</u>

www.politicos.com.news/stories/0710/40433.html

www.ellsberg.net

Plain Dealer 11/20/1969

www.historyplace.com/unitedstates/vietnam/index-1969.html
"The Bitter End 1969-1973"

www.openculture.com, (Getty image)

www.britannica.com/EBchecked/topic/450326/pentagon-papers

www.history.com/topics/vietnam-war/pentagonpapers

www.ejasrevues.org, European Journal of American studies

Turse, Nick, Kill Anything That Moves, Henry Holt & Co ISBN 978-0-8050-8691-1 Picador ISBN 9781250045065, NY, 2013

www.statisticbrain.com/vietnam-war-statistics

www.nytimes.com/2013/10/10/opinion/for-america-life-was-cheap-in-vietnam

www.motherjones.com/mixed-media/2014/02/shirley-temple-dead-85-politics

www.digitalhistory,uh.edu/learning_history/vietnam/vietnam_pubopinion

www.sparknotes.com/history/american/vietnamwar/section8.html

Ambrose, Stephen, "Nixon: The Triumph of a Politician" politicos.com

www.hn.source.com/shotlist/BHC-TV/1969/07/31/BG 4507/405/71

www.armyhistory.org/09/general-maxwell-d-taylor

www.archives.gov/research/pentagon-papers/Report of the Office of the Secretary of Defense Vietnam Task Force

www.nationalguard.mil/1969.aspx

www.ong.ohio.gov/Ohio national guard history, The Ohio Adjunct General's Department

www.articles.courant.com, "National Guard Served Bravely in Vietnam", February 28, 2004

Sebby, Don, SGM(CA) Post Historian Camp San Luis Obispo/Militarymuseum

Snook, David L., The Vietnam Era: History of Iowa National Guard

Ohio History references for Kent State are listed in the text

Chapter 6 College; Hillary Rodham at Wellesley

Cosgrove, Ben, "Life with Hillary": Portraits of a Wellesley Grad, 1969, www.time.com, Feb 15, 2014

www.wellesleycollege.edu, "Remarks of Hillary Rodham's 1969 student commencement speech" Trustees of Wellesley College, Ruth M. Adams, President Wellesley College

www.cbsnews.com, Hilary Rodham's 1969 commencement address-Wellesley College 1969 student commencement speech May 21, 1969, 2007

Kreutz, Liz and Dooley, Erin, "12 moments that define the woman who wants to be President, abcnews.go.com, April 13, 2015.

Life Magazine, Vol.66 Number 24, June 20, 1969. Time, Inc.

Keith, Tamara "5 Things You Should Know about Hillary Clinton", April 11, 2015

Chapter 7 Peace Movement, Civil Rights, Feminism, Protest

<u>Turbulent Years: The 60's</u>, Time Life Books, Alexandria, VA

Jenkins, Philip, <u>Decade of Nightmares: The end of the Sixties and the Making of Eighties America</u>, Oxford University Press, 2006.

Boolt, Dr. Ernest and Garnett, Amanda, Project for Associated Colleges of the South, University of Richmond, facultystaff. richmond.edu/(tilda)ebolt/history398

Afroamhistory.about.com/od/timelines/fl/African-American-History-Timeline-1965-to-1969.htm.

Indiana University Magazine of History: The Other Side of Campus –Young Americans for Freedom

The Daily Californian <u>News: "Life</u> in the Political Closet: A Glimpse into the Berkeley College Republicans"

Kuhistory.com, University of Kansas Prelude to Disorder

Bigalke, Zach, "Student Protests in the University of Oregon Campus: demonstrations of the late 60's. Unbound/special collections and University archives Jan 21, 2015.

Vox, Lisa, AFAM History Expert, "Civil Rights Movement timeline from 1965 to 1969 afroamhistory.about.com

Sa.sc.edu, University of South Carolina Office of Multicultural Student Affairs

www.historyhouse.gov, U House of Representatives, Consequence of changes 1929-1970

Chapter 8 A different Activism: GFWC, Rotary, Lions, Knights of Columbus, charities

Wilson, Linda D., Oklahoma Federation of Women's Clubs" Encyclopedia of Oklahoma History and Culture July 8, 2013

www.archives.chicagotribune.com, Jan 16, 1969

National Association of Colored Women's Clubs, 1968-1982 minutes

Radcliffe College, 1997 New England women's club records

www.mnhs.org/collections/manuscripts/phil.html

rotary.org

lionsclubs.org

lcif.org (lions clubs international foundation0

kofc.org

Statistical Abstract of the United States 1969 funds/Red cross

Hastings-on-Hudson website

Chapter 9 Slang/Music/TV

Kirkpatrick, Rob, <u>1969 The Year That Changed Everything</u>, Skyhorse Publishing 2009 ISBN 9781061239-366-0

1969tv.htm

www.shmoop.com/1960s/culture.htmlwww.citrus.k12.p1.us/staffdev/social%29studippdf/slang%20of%20the%201960's.pdf

www.infoplease.com/year/1969.htm

Ruhlmann, William, www.allmusic.com

www.bobburst.com/popculture

Chapter 10 Woodstock and the Boy Scouts

Epperidge, Bill, "Visual Feast" Woodstock photographs

www.facebook.com/notes/indiana-bible-college/woodstock-lingering-memories-from-the-IBC-perspectives

http://history1900's.about.com/od/1960s/woodstock.htm

Burke, Melissa Nan, ydr.com'c1_13080883

http://usscouts.org/ussouts/history/jambo/1969pictures.asp

Pinterest/Woodstock collection

Chapter 11 seniors

Orr, Richard, www.archives.chicagotribune.com Aug 16 1969, "Senior Citizens whoop it up during Fair's Golden Age Day, Springfield, Illinois Aug 15, 1969

www.icpsr.umich.edu/icpsrweb/icpsr/studies/9780 Issue 19 June-August 1969

George, Linda and Binstock, Robert H. Handbook of Aging and the Social Sciences, Elsevier Publishers Academic Press

Mathis, Evelyn S. "Characteristics of Residents of Nursing and Personal Care Homs United States Department of Health and Human Services Issue 19 June-Aug 1969. National Center for Health Statistics.

www.ncbi.nih.nih.gov Health Services Review

Ann Arbor News, Ann Arbor Michigan Sunday Feb 28, 2016.

www.archives.chicagotribune.com/Sunday May 4, 1969.

"Utilization of Short Stay Hospitals, Annual Summary for the US 1975 US Department of Health Education and Welfare, Data from the National Health Survey, Library of the University of California WZANISI Ser. 13, 1977.

Chapter 12 Cuba Hijackings

Cummings, Dennis "Take this Plane to Cuba": Remembering the hijackings of the 1960's Oct 12, 2009.

www.dangerousminds.net. "You're not on Candid Camera: Allen Funt was on hijacked flight/passengers took it for a prank" October 1, 2003.

www.aviationsafetynetwork

Mikkelson, David M., www.snopes.com, Bonus Smiles: "Investigating the rumor that passengers on an airline diverted to Cuba thought the hijacking was a "Candid Camera" stunt due to the coincidental presence of the show's host Allen Funt"

www.cuban-exile.com

Chapter 13 UFO, Project Blue Book

www.ufoevidence.org, President Jimmy Carter's UFO sighting January 6, 1969 www.nicap.org/waves/1969fullre.htm, "The 1969 UFO Chronology"

www.ufoevidence.org/cases/case294.htm

www.ufoevidence.org/topics/condon.html

Chapter 14 IBM, Big Companies

WatsononTwitter@IBMWatson

www.ibmwatson.com

www.03.ibm.com/innovation/68/watson

www.bloomberg.com/news/2014-01-31/ibm-complaint-to-twitter-leads-to-patent-purchase

www.inventors.about.com/library/weekly/aa091598.htm

www.inventors.aabout.com/od/computersandinternet

Bellis, Mary, http://ibm-history.htm

Kepes, Ben, www.forbes.com, /sites/benkepes/2014/02/03/aws (Amazon)-and-ibm-frankly-they-should-both-just-grow-up

www.smithsonianeducation.org/scitech/carbons/1960.html

www.computerhope.com/history/1960-80.htm

www.computerhostory.org/semiconductor/timeline/1963-ITL.html

www.ranker.com, "Companies Founded in 1969 GNU free document license

Chapter 15 Arpanet

http://www.csucla.edu/about/history/the-day-the-internet-uttered-its-first-words

Professor Leonard Kleinroch, UCLA

Brown, John Seeley. Intel, http://bigthink.com/videos/the-internet-utters-its-first-word

www.history.com/this-day-in-history

Crocker, Stephen D., www.livinginternet.com/internet/history/ARPANET-The-First-Internet

www.computerhistory.org/internethistory

www.inventors.about.com/library/weekly/aa091598.htm

Chapter 16 Vital Statistics

www.famousbirthdays.com/year/VO69p108.htm

www.imbd.com/search/name?birth-year-1969

www.whosdatedwho.com/section/celebrity-divorces/archive/1969

Chapter 17 TV, Toys and Talk Shows

www.imbd.com/title/1400638921

www.tv.com/shows/category/talk-and-interview/decade/1960's

www.sixties60s.com/1969gadgets.htm

www.thepeoplehistory.com/1969toys.html

www.plaidstallions.com/tru/69_html

www.imbd.com/poll/aCibmD(phi)RUE

www.1969tv.htm

www.imbd.com/title/++0063892/Dellaa/1969

www.adland.TV founded by Dabitch 1996

www.superbowlcommercials.tv

www.archives.chicagotribune.com, Wednesday, April 16, 2006

www.huffingtonpostsports.com

www.holidays:thefuntimesguide.com

Gardner, Sean@2morrownight

Chapter 18 Poverty and School Lunches

www.inequalit.org/absolute-poverty-america

www.census.gov/hhas/www/poverty/data/threshold/fhis69.htm.

www.fas/sgp/crs/misc/RL33069.pdf, 11-13-13

Gabe, Thomas, Congressional Record Service–Poverty in US, 2012

www.fns.usda.gov, Child Nutrition Tables

Collier, Andrea King, www.nationalgeographic.com, "the plate" / Black Panthers, November 4, 2015

Milkman, Arielle, www.eater.com, "The Radical Origins of Free Breakfast for Children", February 16, 2016

Chapter 19 River fire, Oil Spill, Alcatraz

www.epa.gov/compliance/nepa

www.history.com/this-day-in-history/explosion-rocks-USS Enterprise

Corwin, Miles, LT Times Jan.28, 1989, www.thinkprogress.org/oil-spill-heard-round-the-world

www.nbcnews.com, "1969 oil spill near Santa Barbara was galvanizing for the environmental organization"

www.silcom.com/wsbven/spill/sbhtml.

Adler, Jonathon H. Washington Post, The Volokh Conspiracy "The Fable of the Burning River–45 years later".

www.ohiohistorycentral.org/w/Cuyahoga-River-Fire Feb. 24, 2015

www.time.com/3921976/Cuyahoga-fire June 22, 2015

Ross, Alexa, researcher. NVdatabaseswarthmore.edu, "Native Americans Occupy Alcatraz for land rights" 10/23/2010

www.nepis.epa.gov/USEnvironmental–Protection–Agency Radiological Health Laboratory US Department of Health Education and Welfare Public Health.

Dallas Services Group of Texas Instruments Inc. corporate author "Final Report of off-site surveillance for the Milrow event Oct 2, 1996"

Chapter 20 Tax

www.irs.gov/pub/irs-501/tehistory.pdf

www.mnhs.org/collections/manuscript/phil.html

http://ir.lawnet.fordhan.edu/egi/viewcontent.cgi?article=2039&content-flr&se-redir=1&refrer=

www.americaforthe arts.org/b-program/reports-and-data/legislation-policy/legislation

www.aam-us.org American Alliance of Museums

Chapter 21 Guns

www.abcnew.go.com/us/story?ide93456

Cosgriff, Chris, "Officer Down Memorial Page", www.odmp.org, 1996–2016

Cline, Seth, US News, "US Gov't Tried to Tackle Gun Violence in the 1960's, 1/16/2013

www.OJJGP.gov/pubs Report

www.vintageadsandstuff.com/rifleman-1969, American Rifleman magazines

www.smartgunlaws.org 2012

NiftyNYC http://www.niftynyc.com/events/sunday-september-21s-law-and-order-1969-discussed-with-documentarian-frederick-wiseman 9-21-2014

Chapter 22 Future Billionaires

Holm, Erik, Wall Street Journal, "Money Beat", www.blogswsj.com, May 2, 2015 7:24 a.m.

www.forbes.com, "The World's Billionaires (Gates/Buffet/Trump)

www.biography.com/people/oprah-winfrey 9884419

ibid/steve-jobs-9354805

ibid/bill-gates-9307520

ibid/warren-buffet-9230729

www.entrepreneur.com, "Sam Walton, Bargain Basement Billionaire"

ibid/"Steve Jobs: An Extraordinary Career"

www.corporate.walmart.com/our-story-our-history/Walmart

www.sec.gov/d262056dex41.htm, "Restated certificate of incorporation of Wal-Mart Stores, Inc.

www.notablebiographies.com, Steve Jobs biography

www.allaboutstevenjbs.com, timeline 1955-1985

www.trump.com

Barbaro, Michael, NYTimes shared from www.seattletimes.com, originally published September 8, 2015, "Trump unveiled in New Biography (called Never Enough: Donald Trump and the Pursuit of Success)

Chapter 23 Weather

www.weatherhistory.findthebest.com/d/6/1969/mg

ibid/findthebad.com/d/6/1969/mg

Farmers Almanac, July 20, 1969

www.underground.com/hurricane/at1969.asp

www.weatherspark.com/history/3108/1969/New-York-United-States, April 2007

www.cityroom.blogs.nytimes.com/2009/02/10/remembering-a-snowstorm-that-paralyzed-the-city, Sewell 2/10/09

www.nola.com and www.wundergound.com (refute the hurricane party story at the Richlieu apartments in Pass Christian)

Chapter 24 Farms

Ganzell, Bill, The Gazette Group, "Wessels living history: Farming in the 50's and 60's. www.livinghistoryfarm.org

Pherson, Carl L., Thomas, Kenneth H., and Nodland, Truman R. www.purl.umn.edu/8501, University of Minnesota, Department of Applied Economics: Economic Study Reports/Specialized dairy farms in southern Minnesota 1968-69.

USDA Historical Archive Vol. 2 1969 census, "Farms: number, use of land, size of farm. www.usda.mannlib.com.edu

www.naldc.nat.usda.gov, "Major Uses of Land in the United States–Summary for 1969. Agricultural Economic Report #247

www.aphis.usda.gov, "Pigs", timeline of events

Statistical Abstract of the United States, US Department of Commerce Publications B 753972 92nd annual edition

www.champpull.org/history.html

www.ntpapull.com

Communes

Strauss, Marcia, "An archaeologist excavates a Hippie Commune preserved in 1969 by Fire", 6/18/2008

www.americanhistory.si.edu, "Communal Living 1969

Spiegel, Alison, food writer and editor, www.huffingtonpost.com, "Peace, Love, and Granola: The Untold Story of the Food Shortage at Woodstock"

www.bibl-archive.library.yale.edu, "American and the Utopian Dream"/Hog Farm

Brown, Dana, <u>Back to the Land: the Enduring Dream of Self-sufficiency in Modern America</u>, University of Wisconsin Press

Chapter 25 Flower Children

Boston, Bernie. www.washingtonpost.com from Washington Evening Star

Brown, Dona, <u>Back to the Land: The Enduring Dream of Self-sufficiency in Modern America</u>, University of Wisconsin Press, pp. 206–211/

Brownlee, John. www.fastcodesign.com, "Why This Vintage He-Man Action Figure Still Smells Bad 30 Years Later"

Cumberdale, Hubert, www.proflowers.com, "Flower Power and the Sixties.

Erickson, Hal, From Beautiful Downtown Burbank: A Critical History of Rowan and Martin's Laugh-in, McFarland & Co. Jefferson, NC, ISBN 978-0-7869-40498

Nov. 2010

Stone, Skip, www.hipplanet.com, "Hippies from A to Z

www.he-man.org/Stinkor

www.herbs.yuku.co/topic/3653743/why-patchouli-oil-is-associated-with-hippies, Nov. 9 2007

www.iconicphotos.wordpress.com

www.imbd.com, Laugh-in episode #3.6, 1960

www.megaessays.cm/viewpaper/35794.gtml, "Influences on Body Art Essays"

www.tvacres.com

www.urbandictionary.com/define.php?item=patchouli

Chapter 26 Guitar and Sitars

www.articls.latimes.com, "In 1969, singer recorded the first Christian rock album"

www.ravishankar.org

www.biography.com, Ravi Shankar

Clark, Sue, Rolling Stone Magazine, "Ravi Shankar: The Rolling Stone Interview" March 9, 1968

Hamel, Paul, Archive of the Ministry International Journal for Pastors, July 1973

Giesecke, www.archiveschicagotribune.com April 24, 1969

Chapter 27 Education

www.census.gov, US Department of Commerce Publication, "Population Characteristics/ School Enrollment October 1969, October 1970

www.highered.nysed.gov

Hoachlander, E. Gareth, Kaufman, Phillip and Levesque, Karen, MPR Associates, Inc., National Center for Education Statistics Compendium of Statistics "Vocational Education in the United States 1969-1990, February. 1992

www.npr.org, "The Legacy of School Busing", April 39, 2004.

www.wsj.com, Wall Street Journal, "Chicago Teachers Strike Over Funding" updates April 1, 2016

www.northcarolinahistory.org, "Swann v. Charlotte-Mecklenburg Board of Education, written by North Carolina History Project 2016 and The John Locke Foundation

www.dailykos.com, "First Teachers Union Strike"

Berlin, Jonathon, contact reporter, March 31, 2016, 5:05 p.m.

www.archive.chicagotribune.com, March 9, 1969 Sunday Section

Gray, Julie Salley, "To Fight the Good Fight: The Battle over Control of the Pasadena City Schools 1969-1979

www.bostonglobe.com, "Busing: An Oral History"

www.carolinahistory.web.unc.edu, Charlotte, NC: Birthplace (and Place od Death) of Integration in Public School"

Staples, I. Ezra, Associate Superintendent for Instructional Services, SD of Philadelphia, www.ascd.org, "The Open-Space Plan in Education"

www.openculture.com, "Mr. Rogers Goes to Congress and Saves PBS, video, October 26, 2015.

Benson, Sonia, Brannen, Daniel E. Jr, and Valentine, Rebecca, US History in Context: Busing for School Desegregation, UXL Encyclopedia of US History, Vol.1 UXL 2009 216-21, Web April 25, 2016.

www.nyc.gov, "The History of Open Admissions and Remedial Education at the City University of New York.

Thomas, Jacqueline Rabe, www.ctmmirror.org, "60 Years after Brown vs. Board of Education: Still separate in Connecticut", June 28, 2014.

www.fas.org, Congressional Record Service, Glenn J McLaughlin, Section Research Manager and Mark Gurevitz, Information Research Specialist, January 7, 2014.

Harris, Alisha, www.slate.com, from Browbeat, Slate's culture blog, October 5, 2012.

Bradberry, Travis, www.forbes.com/leadership, "How Emotional Intelligence Landed Mr. Rogers $20 million. September 5, 2014.

Chapter 28 Religion

Newport, Frank, www.gallup.com, "Questions and Answers about American Religion, December 24, 2007'Gallup, George Jr., George H. Gallup International Institute, "Catholics Trail Protestants in Church Attendance"

www.beattlesbible.com

www.mum.edu/marhareshimaheshyogi

Hughes, Richard, Buddhism in America, Columbia University Press, Cambridge p. 142

www.shambala.com

(Sites listed under charities such as emptytomb.org and cjp.org were used here as well)

Chapter 29 Inventors and Scientists

Leung, Isaac, https://www.electronicnews.com.au, October 22, 2012

Feder,BarnabyJ.,www.nytimes.com/standfor-ovshinsky-an-inventor-compared-to-edison-dies-at-89, October19, 2012 (author corrects hybrid to hydride in update)

Gordon-Bloomfield, Nikki, www.greencarreports.com>new>EV, October 19, 2012

"Statistical Abstract of the U.S., U.S. Department of Commerce Publications B752972, 92nd Edition, 1971

Jena, Dunham G, www.blackpast.org, "Creating the Heating System for Radio City Music Hall NYC"

www.energyquest.ca.gov

www.computerhistory.org/semi-conductor/timeline/1963-TTL.html

www.inventors.about.com>...>famous-inventors-I to J/Intel

www.content.edlib.org,"BipolarRAM1969"/ark:/1303/kt65202131?layout=metadata

www.biography.com/people/george-caruthers/536794

Bellis, Mary, www.about.com/inventors

Kelly,Kate,www.americacomesalive.com/maria-van-brittan-brown-home-security-system-inventor, 2014

Statistical Abstract of the United States 92nd edition, part 8, p. 526, Scientists by Scientific Field 1969, pub 1971. www.cenus.gov/library/publications 1971

Statistical Abstract of the United States, 93rd edition, Patents and trademarks filed p.530, pub 1972.

www.antarcticsun.usap.gov/features/content-handbook, Nov 13, 2009

www.usnews.com/Forty-Years-of-Women-in-Antartica

Antarctic Journal of the United States, www.documents.library.net.gov, Vol V, Number 4, July–August 1970, U.S. Antarctic Research Program 1969-70 Part 1 Summer Session.

www.exploatorium.edu, "Origins Antarctica"

Tidbits references are in order of appearance in the text, not alphabetically

Kolata, Gina, www.nytimes.com/.../boys-1969-death-suggests-aids-invaded-US. October 28,1989

Hunter,Al,www.weeklyview.net/2014/05/08/robert-rayford-america's-first-aids-victim
www.history-computers.com/GaryStarkweather

www.historyofinformation.com, May 13, 2016

www.kentuckyderby.com/history/year/1969, 2016

www.horseracingnation.com/race/1969/kentucky-derby

www.annemace.net. "Snapshots in Time" www.dogwoodlonerambles.blogspot.com, Wed July 25, 2012

www.recipelink.com, The Kitchen Link 1995

www.tasteofhome.com/greenbeansalad

www.ranker.com.list/defunct-retailers-in-the-US

www.departmentstorehistory.net/disc.htm

www.thedepartmentstoremuseum.org

Cosgriff, Chris

www.officerdown.com. Memorial Page

www.history.com/this-day-in-history, June-28-1969

www.thestonewallinnyc.com

Archer, Jules, The Incredible Sixties: The Stormy Years That Changed America, Harcourt, Brace, Jovanevich, 1986

www.news.hrvh.org, "Historied" Newspapers Number 8, edition 91, April 4, 1986

www.lambek.net, comiclopedia

www.scientology.org

www.cchr.org, A Report by Concerned Citizens on Human Rights, Issue 2, June 2006

https://www.cs.cmu.edu/dist/E-meter/courtfile-2-69.html, "The Founding Church of Scientology of Washington, D.C. et. Al. Appellants v. the United States 1969 Appellee no. 21483

www.epa.gov/.../ddt-regulatory DDT Regulatory History: A Brief Survey to 1975, Report, and July 1975

www.infoplease.com/year/1969.html

www.livinghistoryfarm.org/farminginthe 50s/pests_.09.html

www.amhistory.si.edu/archives/AC06SI.pdf, Smithsonian Institution

Minnik, Mimi, www.amhistory.si.edu/archives/d7651.htm, July 1998, revised Jan 2, 2012

www.archives.chicagotribune.com, Newark, NJ (AP), June 26, 1987

www.peabody.yale.edu/../deinonychus-antirrhopus-os. 2016

www.cod.edu, Dinosaur Revolution, Lynn's page, 2000

Conniff, Richard, www.yalealumnimagazine.com, "The Man Who Saved The Dinosaurs" July/August 2014

www.peabody.yale.edu/.../deinonychus-antirrhyeus-05, 2016

www.museum.cornell.edu, Andrew Dickson White Museum of Art in 1969

Larsen, Lars B. www.macba.cat/.../04-earth-art-eng.pdf, November 8, 2010

www.dancetheatreofharlem.org/legacy

www.infoplease.com>literatureandthe arts>performing arts>dance, Columbia Press 2012

www.nps.gov/kala/learn.../a-brief-history-of-kalaupapa, National Park Service 2016

Ross, Phillip, www.ibtimes.com, "Kalaupapa, Hawaii Leper Colony: A Look inside The Remote Island for the State's Few Surviving Leprosy Patients", April 5, 2015, 2:34 p.m.

Further Reading suggested but not necessarily endorsed

Vietnam:

Arnett, Peter, <u>Live From The Battlefield</u>, From Vietnam to Bagdad, 35 Years in the World's Worst War Zones, A Touchstone Book published by Simon and Shuster, 1995, ISBN 0-671-75586-2

Kerrey, Robert J., <u>When I Was A Young Man, A Memoir, Harcourt. Inc.</u> 2002

Palmer, Laura, <u>Shrapnel In The Heart</u>, Letters and Remembrances from the Vietnam Veterans Memorial, Random House, Vintage Books, New York, 1988

Hurricane Camille:

Ellis, Dan, <u>All About Camille.</u> Published on Amazon July 2000 revised 2010

Related to 1969:

Kilpatrick, Rob, <u>1969 The Year That Changed Everything</u>, Skyline Publications 2009, ISBN 978-1-60239-366-0

Rosen, Roth, <u>The World Split Open,</u> How the Women's Movement Changed America, Viking/Penguin Press, 2000

Horn, Miriam, <u>Rebels in White Gloves</u>, First Anchor Books/Random House, 1999 ISBN 0-385-720184

Time Life Books, <u>Turbulent Years the 60's,</u> Alexandria VA

Reich, Charles A., <u>The Greening of America</u>, Random House, 1970

Stone, Skip, www.hipplanet.com, "Hippies from A to Z"

Wessels livinghistoryfarm.org, Farming in the 59's and 60's, A living history from York Nebraska by Bill Ganzel, The Gazette Group, 2007

www.ingramcontent.com/pod-product-compliance
Lightning Source LLC
LaVergne TN
LVHW011947070526
838202LV00054B/4835